Happy Birthday Karen
July - 27 - 1956

From Auntie
Florence

THE COLT
from
HORSE HEAVEN HILLS

BY ELEANOR F. BROWN

Illustrated by Pers Crowell

JULIAN MESSNER, INC.
New York

Published by Julian Messner, Inc.

8 West 40th Street, New York 18

Published simultaneously in Canada
by the Copp Clark Company, Ltd.

©Copyright 1956 by Eleanor F. Brown

Library of Congress Catalog Card No. 56–6785

PRINTED IN THE UNITED STATES OF AMERICA

FOR
HELEN

———————

BOOKS BY ELEANOR F. BROWN

The Colt from Horse Heaven Hills
A Horse for Peter
Wendy Wanted A Pony

CONTENTS

THE COLT
FROM HORSE HEAVEN HILLS

CHAPTER I

Peter Gets a Phone Call

The wild black colt snorted in terror. His breath came in shuddering gasps and his nostrils flared red in the darkness as he tried desperately to keep his balance in the big, swaying stock truck. Legs braced, he stood tense and quivering; but the sharp curves in the road threw him repeatedly against the tight-packed, sweaty bodies of the other horses.

Inside the cab the driver's companion spoke dubiously as the rickety truck careened around an especially bad turn. "Ain't you steppin' on the gas pretty hard, Bill? Them horses gonna be pretty skinned up time we hit the stockyards."

The burly driver spat in disgust. "Who cares? Bunch of no-account broomtails goin' to a killer plant don't have to be wrapped in no cotton wool. I'm dog-tired, and we're 'way late with this load."

The first speaker shrugged. The truck sped wildly on through the night. The black three-year-old knew only stark, unreasoning fear. Something tremendous and different had snatched him from the barren hills of his birth and thrust him abruptly into this lurching, bumpy prison, but he had no way of knowing what or why. Just five days before, he had been running with a wild herd—one of several such that roamed the Horse Heaven country of south central Washington. The young stallion was extremely well developed for a three-year-old. Strong and rough-coated, he was nevertheless clean-limbed and fine-boned with a general air of quality that set him apart from the rest of the herd. He alone had been able to hold his own against the gray leader and thus stay with them. Several times he had even challenged the gray's supremacy and, had the band been allowed to roam unmolested, he would sooner or later have become its acknowledged leader.

But riders had come and driven them into a narrow, rock-walled canyon with a sheer cliff blocking the end. Once inside and cornered, the wild herd had been held by shouting horsemen on quick, cat-like cowponies, until barbed wire had been strung up to cut off their escape.

After three days they were driven into quickly assembled loading chutes, packed tightly into open-racked trucks, and started on the long, winding road along the Columbia River to Portland. The black's mother had gone with the first load, but the young stallion had persistently eluded his captors and was among the very last driven into the chute.

It was raining when the fleet of trucks unloaded at the big, sprawling stockyards which, with two packing plants, covered a forty-acre plot. The wild horses were shunted into high, muddy corrals flanked by bawling cattle and smelly sheep. The mud thrown up by churning hoofs crusted their shaggy coats, already damp with sweat, and they huddled miserably in the downpour, awaiting the coming of dawn.

The early-morning light broke through the heavy clouds with stubborn persistence as the packing-plant roustabouts filled the watering troughs and threw a pile of soggy hay into each corral. The black stood a little apart, his head proudly erect. In spite of the mud, sweat, and weariness he was arrogant and beautiful. His legs were shapely, his hoofs small. The slender, crested neck, fine head, and well-sprung barrel were a sharp contrast to the thick necks, coarse heads, and mediocre bodies that marked so many of the herd. Even the handlers, who drove dozens of horses in and out each day, stopped to give the black a second look.

As the day wore on, the news of something unusual spread from chute to chute; and finally the yard superintendent, a lean, gray-eyed man in stockman's pants and cowboy boots, threaded his way among the maze of corrals, seeking the black. Thrusting his hat back on his head, he planted a foot on the lower fence rail and keenly appraised the stallion. His gray eyes warmed in appreciation; then he turned to one of the nearby handlers.

"That fellow's no product of scrub stock. Some rancher's blooded stud horse must have gotten loose and run with that wild herd for a spell, or maybe this colt was bred on a ranch and got loose. He's either purebred or sired by a mighty fine stallion. Just to look at him, I'd say that colt's half Thoroughbred." He shook his head regretfully. "Sure hate to see him killed. For that matter, there's three or four in this shipment might make good saddle horses or jumpers. Noticed 'em as I came down the line. Guess I'll call Jerry."

Looking thoughtful, the superintendent walked to the office, seized the phone, and dialed a number.

✿   ✿   ✿

"Hey, Peter! Telephone!"

Peter Morgan brought Star, his prize Tennessee walking stallion, to an abrupt stop. His warm, brown eyes questioned the trim figure in whipcords that had suddenly appeared at the door of the West Hills Riding Academy indoor ring.

"O.K., Dad. Who is it?"

"Jerry Harper. He says it's urgent."

A quick smile swept across the clean-cut features topped with a shock of dark, unruly hair and finished off with a square-set jaw and determined chin. Peter eased himself slowly down from the saddle, using the special leather bracket on the front. He handed Star's reins to his father and hurried toward the door, moving with a noticeable limp. In the office he draped

[14]

his tall, slender figure over a chair and picked up the phone.

"Hi, Jerry. It's me."

Jerry's voice was crisp. "I have a hurry-up call to go see some horses. If you'd like to go, be ready on the double."

"Did I ever turn down a chance to look at horses—especially with you? Just give the usual signal with the horn when you drive up."

Peter hurried to the house to tell his mother where he was going, gave his tousled hair a lick and promise with a wet comb, then rushed back to the ring. John Morgan was just putting the black into the long, gliding walk for which the Tennessee walker is famous. Peter watched proudly. Star was his own horse, a very special gift on his thirteenth birthday a year ago, from the people of Glen Valley, the small town from which the Morgans had moved to the city only two months before. Peter's father had been a part-time trainer for a private show stable there, as well as a fruit grower; but when the chance came to buy at a bargain a run-down riding academy in the city where he had lived as a boy, he could not resist the challenge. He now rented, boarded, and trained horses, besides teaching elementary and advanced riding.

Peter's attention was suddenly diverted from Star by three sharp blasts from Jerry's horn. He jumped into the cab of the truck and settled down beside his father's old friend with curious anticipation.

"Where we going, Jerry?"

"Wait and see."

Peter knew it was no use to question further. Jerry ran a berry farm near the city, but he made a hobby of buying young bargain horses, unbroken but promising, and breaking them for the fun of it. Then he sold them, for very little more than he had paid, to people who couldn't otherwise afford a horse. He and Peter had developed a real friendship in the short time the Morgans had been in Portland.

Jerry suddenly turned to Peter with a grin. "Think any horse could ever replace Star in your affections? Now that he's no longer shown and is kept mainly for stud, I'm wondering if you don't need a new interest."

Peter flashed back at him indignantly. "Another horse replace Star? I should say not! I'd wanted a horse all my life, before I got him, and I'll never forget the night he was given to me. Besides, he's a grand horse—one in a million. You know that as well as I do, Jerry."

"Don't get excited," Jerry admonished. "I just wondered. If I were in your place I'd feel the same. After all, Pete, that was a pretty swell thing you did, pulling little Ann Woods out from under the wheels of that runaway truck. Look how many months you were in the hospital and a wheel chair as a result. No wonder the people of Glen Valley bought you Star as a birthday present. By the way, notice any improvement in your hip these last few weeks?"

"A little," Peter told him.

Now there was only the lameness, with occasional pain and tenderness in the bad joint to remind him of what had been like a bad dream. He had to take it pretty easy though when it came to twisting his body suddenly, and he grew impatient and angry at times because his father would not let him ride the more difficult horses at the Academy.

"Can't take a chance," John Morgan always said. "We all sweat blood getting you this well, and we're not going to have you laid up again."

"I'd like to be able to train," Peter said glumly. "You know, Jerry, after I got hurt, Doc Bush said I could never be a trainer like Dad. All I can do is ride—gentle horses like Star—and draw pictures of other people's gaited horses. That helps some."

Suddenly Jerry turned off in the direction of the packing plant. Peter's heart sank. His friend too often liked to look over the horses that were brought in for butchering.

"Look!" Peter's voice was determined. "You know how I feel about that packing plant. It's bad enough— those horses being killed—without me having to see them first. The one time I went with you before, it bothered me for days."

"I know, but I told you I had a very special reason

[17]

for wanting you to go this time. I don't like it out here any better than you do, but every horse I buy is just one less killed. Look at it that way. And remember that every bad winter a lot of wild horses die of slow starvation out on the range. This is a quick way out."

They rode along in silence. Peter was disappointed. He had hoped they were going out into the open country. When they entered the packing-plant gates and headed for the corrals, he tried not to look at the horses milling around inside.

Jerry finally found the office. The gray-eyed superintendent came out smiling, was introduced as Tom Wilson, and shook hands. Getting into the cab, he directed them to the very end of the yard.

"We've got the five or six head in here that I thought might interest you," he explained. "You can have any of 'em at just what we'd get from the packing plant—three cents a pound."

Jerry jumped out. "Thanks for calling, Tom. Come on, Pete. I want your opinion on these."

Peter knew he was being flattered, but he followed Jerry over to the fence. "You don't need anybody's advice when it comes to horses," he said dryly.

"Thanks!" Jerry's eyes suddenly lighted on the black three-year-old. He turned to Tom Wilson. "That was why you wanted us to come, wasn't it?"

The superintendent nodded. "Yep, but these others aren't too bad either."

Then Peter saw the black. He swallowed hard and turned away.

But, irresistibly, his gaze was drawn back. He saw the fear and desolation in the dark eyes, mingled with a strange, proud defiance. Pity rose up, sharp and burning, in Peter's throat and chest. At the same moment the colt, whether by accident or intent, took a step toward him and looked him full in the eye. It was almost as if he were begging for help.

Peter turned. "Jerry, buy him . . . please!"

"I told you I wanted you to come for a very special reason. This horse *is* different. Tom told me over the phone. Remember he's wild stock, green off the range. He'll need months of careful gentling, and he needs a light rider . . . like you maybe. I haven't much time right now, and I'm far from light. I'll buy him for you if your Dad will let you keep him at the Academy. I'm sure this black is basically gentle and sensible, but if he should turn out to be an outlaw I'll take him off your hands later."

Peter gulped. He looked at the colt again. He spoke to him, his voice soothing and coaxing. The black's ears pricked forward. He looked curious. The boy kept on talking. The stallion took another short, tentative step forward; then, startled at a sudden movement, he leaped back.

"Come on, fellow. If I had you, I'd call you Ebony. . . . No! Charcoal! Ebony's too common."

The colt came almost to the fence, a foot or so at

[19]

a time; but when Peter put out a tentative hand he drew back. In the meantime Jerry sized up the other horses and decided on three of them.

"Well?" he turned to Peter. "What do you say? You can tell he likes you."

Peter wanted the black desperately. The very mystery of his origin, the chance to work carefully with him and see what the outcome would be, appealed to him. But there were two obstacles. His heart sank as he realized they were mighty big ones.

"Look, Jerry. It's swell of you, but I won't let you *give* me a present like that. If *I* had thirty dollars it would be different. And *if* we lived on a farm again and the price of hay and grain weren't out of sight, that would be different too. I know Dad won't hear of it."

"Well, let's go telephone him," Jerry insisted. "It won't do any harm."

Doubtfully Peter followed him to the office. He knew the struggle his father was having to make the Riding Academy pay its way. Business hadn't picked up as he had hoped. It wouldn't do to have an extra horse eating its head off and earning nothing. Still Peter's mind began racing wildly, trying to think of ways he could earn extra money toward the colt's keep.

When John Morgan answered, Jerry told him the story briefly and persuasively.

"I think this black has possibilities, John. There's Thoroughbred blood there, or I'm a cockeyed cowpoke. Can't you find a corner for him somewhere and let the boy see what he can do with him? After all, Peter's a trainer's son."

Peter knew by the look on Jerry's face that his father had said no, but his friend kept on trying.

"Don't be silly, John. Look at all you've done for me, particularly in the old days. You know I can spare the money." Jerry hesitated, listening. "O.K., I'll let you talk to the boy. Really thought I had a good idea there."

Peter took the phone. He was surprised to find his father did not sound angry.

"Now what's this all about? If there are any horses bought around here, I'm buying them—not Jerry. Jerry doesn't owe us any favors. How do you think we can afford to feed a colt that won't earn a cent?"

Peter's heart leaped. He knew from his father's tone there was hope. "How much would his feed cost? I'll take all the care of him and help more with the other horses too."

There was a long silence. Peter held his breath.

"Oh, about eighteen a month, I guess—the way I buy my feed in big quantities. But it's a crazy notion. You've no idea how the horse will turn out. He's just a wild broomtail—a scrub bronc."

"Jerry's a good judge, Dad. You've said so yourself many times. This horse isn't any scrub. You ought to see him."

"W-e-l-l." John Morgan spoke dubiously. "I don't

know when you'll ever get time for him, with all your chores and schoolwork. Understand one thing from the start. You're not to try to ride him till he's completely broken . . . and gentle. Lame as you are, you're not physically able to break any bucking broncos—and you know it. I'll decide *when* and *if* you can ride him."

Peter's heart took a sudden lift. "You mean it's all right? I can have him?"

"Well, we'll try it. But no fussing if he has to go later. And Jerry isn't paying for him. Put him back on the phone."

Peter handed Jerry the phone. His eyes were shining. He turned and hurried back to the corral. The black colt looked at him and moved slowly toward the fence. There was something between them—something real and strong, like the feeling between him and Star. He knew he had not made a mistake.

CHAPTER II

Trailer Troubles

Jerry gazed at the colt, and scratched his head. "Now the fun commences. These wild broomtails will hate the sight of a truck by now. We'll have to load your horse in last, because we'll be taking him off first."

He backed the truck up to a corral—one with a loading chute. Peter watched, fascinated, as two of the mounted yardmen deftly drove the four horses through connecting gates into the chosen corral, separated Jerry's three and forced them up the chute and into the truck. The black stood, proud and aloof, warily watching the riders.

Jerry got down from the cab and came over to Peter. "Been thinking about your horse, Pete. We can't load him with these three. We'd never get him unloaded at your place without the others breaking out too. Minute that end gate goes down, there'd be a mad scramble of horseflesh. It wouldn't matter so much if the truck was backed up to my loading corral or to a bank in one of my pastures, but it would sure be a mess if this bunch got loose at your Dad's ritzy Riding Academy. Much as I hate to put you off, I'd better take this load home; then we'll get your Dad's closed trailer and come back."

"O.K." Peter saw the wisdom of Jerry's words, but he hated going off without his horse.

"We'll be back after the other one tonight," Jerry told the manager.

Peter was unusually thoughtful all the way home. He wished desperately he could have bought the black himself. Somehow it didn't seem right for someone else, even his own father, to own the colt and have all the say about him. Peter racked his brains for money-making ideas. Once he had thought of a paper route, but his lameness prevented that. He sighed. Surely something would turn up.

When Jerry and Peter went in to find John Morgan, he was giving a lesson. They had to interrupt to ask about the trailer.

"It's not here." He spoke a trifle impatiently. "Don't you remember, Pete, that I let the Johnsons take their two horses to the ranch in it? They won't be back till tomorrow morning."

Peter's face fell. He *had* forgotten. "Could we bring the black alone in your truck?" he asked Jerry anxiously. "After you've unloaded your horses?"

"I hardly think it's safe. He's of a different mettle from these others. We couldn't tie him in the truck, since he's not halter- or rope-broken. Coming from the range, he was packed in so tight he couldn't have jumped out or banged himself up much—and he had companionship. Alone and scared, he might try to climb the sides. In your Dad's closed trailer he'd be O.K. We'll just have to wait, Pete."

John Morgan gave Jerry his check and then went on about his business. Peter would have liked to explain all about the black and the feeling that had sprung up between them, but his father was too busy to listen. He turned away, disappointed, and went up to the house, a hundred feet or so away from the stable, on the edge of a wooded canyon.

As Peter stepped into the kitchen, warm, spicy odors enveloped him; and his mother turned smilingly toward him, holding out a plate of freshly baked cookies. Mrs. Morgan was a comfortable, kindly sort of person. Her eyes were blue; her hair was slightly gray and naturally wavy. Her voice was soft and welcoming.

"You're just in time. What are you looking so worried about? What's this I hear about your getting a new horse?"

Good old Mom! *She'd* listen to him. Peter flung himself into a chair, grabbed a handful of cookies, and between bites began to tell her all about it. The words tumbled out so fast they almost tripped over each other.

"Well," Mrs. Morgan remarked thoughtfully when

he had finished, "I think you're taking on a lot, but it's all right with me as long as your father approves and you don't take any foolish chances. Don't neglect Star, son. After all, he was your first love. But you *do* need a new interest. I think you've been somewhat lonely since we came to the city. I'll bet your friend Dodo back in Glen Valley would be interested in hearing about this horse."

"Say, she sure will! I'll write tonight."

Peter felt better. Nevertheless all that evening he worried about the black colt, wishing he already had him safely at home. "I'm going to name him Charcoal," he told his parents. "He's black as coal, with a white blaze down his face and an odd little white patch on his nose. Golly, but he's pretty!"

When the Johnsons finally brought back the trailer the next day, it was nearly noon. Peter rushed to the phone and called Jerry. He had hoped his father would offer to go so he wouldn't have to bother his friend; but Saturday was a busy day at the Academy and no one could be spared, particularly Mr. Morgan. It was nearly one when Peter and Jerry finally arrived at the packing plant. They had no trouble getting into the grounds, but the superintendent was nowhere around.

"The office closes at noon on Saturday, and we don't do much over the week end," one of the men said. "But maybe I can help you."

Jerry explained about the black colt. The man looked surprised.

"Didn't know there was anything left from that shipment. Thought you took out what you wanted. The rest of that batch of wild ones went under the knife this noon."

Peter gasped. Before he could say a word, Jerry grabbed his arm.

"The black colt couldn't possibly have been taken," he said quickly. "Tom knew we'd be picking him up, and we bought and paid for him yesterday." He turned to the attendant. "See, here's the receipt. The horse was for the boy here."

The man scanned the paper. "Sure enough. You bought him right enough, but I swear there's nothing left in this section. Take a look for yourself."

With fast-beating heart Peter followed Jerry down the line of corrals. They were empty! For a moment Peter couldn't talk. Then anger and disappointment welled up in him so strongly he had to bite his lip to keep back the bitter words.

Jerry was still unbelieving. "He's got to be somewhere," he said sharply. "Tom wouldn't let us down like that—at least not intentionally. Isn't there someone else around who'll know something definite?"

"Like I told you, we've got a short crew week ends; but I'll go see what I can find out. If the horse is gone, you can know it was a mistake, mister, and you'll get your money back."

Peter swallowed angrily.

"Pretty stupid mistake if he really is gone," Jerry snapped. "And it's not the money we care about. Can't you see the boy really wanted the horse? Find out all you can right away, will you?"

The attendant went off among the maze of corrals. Jerry looked at Peter and turned away. Peter felt too miserable to talk. It seemed hours before the man came back. Peter saw him and went to meet him eagerly.

"Well?"

"We caught him just in time!" The man smiled broadly. "The boys got crossed up. They herded him in with the killer horses all right. Five minutes more and he'd have been a goner. We shunted him back into Corral Number Seven, if you want to load him out."

Peter let out his breath in a gasp of relief. The sights and sounds of the place sickened him. All he wanted was to get his horse and get away from there as quickly as possible. Jerry followed him almost on the run to the corral. Sure enough, there was the black. When he saw them coming he stopped his frenzied circling of the fence and stood eying them suspiciously, head flung high, nostrils dilated—a magnificent picture in spite of the coltish awkwardness which still clung to his rangy frame.

Jerry whistled. "Give him two years more, and he'll take a prize in any beauty show. Well, now we have to get him into the trailer—somehow."

While Jerry backed it right up to the corral gate, Peter talked to the black. The horse quit snorting and stood looking at him curiously, remembering. After a bit he began circling the corral at a walk, coming closer and closer to the fence each time. The third time around, Peter almost touched him with his outstretched hand. He watched the colt carefully, ready to pull his hand away if the black laid back his ears and made a lunge. Even though a strong bond of kinship seemed already to have sprung up between them, the colt had been through a trying ordeal and was still frightened.

By the time Jerry had the trailer in place, Peter was inside the enclosure. He leaned back against the gate, watching the black but making no effort to approach him. The horse studied him carefully, advancing, then falling back. Jerry slowly let down the tail gate of the trailer—after opening the corral just far enough to give access to it, with no space left on either side.

"Lucky it's low to the ground," he said. "Lucky too that I thought to bring some oats. Don't hurry him. Let's try the come-on trick. It's a sure thing we'll never get a rope or halter on him without help."

Jerry reached into the trailer for a sack and put a little heap of oats on the ground ten or fifteen feet inside the corral. Several other little heaps were laid a foot or two apart, with one just where the tail gate touched the ground. Still another and bigger pile went onto the tail gate itself, more on the floor of the trailer, and a final pile in the feed box at the front.

Motioning to Peter to circle slowly around behind the colt, Jerry did so himself from the opposite direction. The black moved toward the trailer to get away from them; then, as they stood unmoving, he relaxed a little and sniffed at the oats. In a moment he was eating them greedily, almost oblivious of their presence. For days he had eaten almost nothing, and oats were a new and delightful treat. The two remained completely immovable, watching the colt closely. Then a sound in a nearby corral startled him. He threw up his head and stood trembling. He whirled about as if to check on Jerry and Peter, then lowered his head to follow the trail of oats.

Peter held his breath. The colt had eaten the pile at the edge of the tail gate. He reached for the one on the tail gate itself; then he put a tentative hoof on the planks, smelling the oats ahead. The boards gave a little, and the metal chain that hung beneath clanked against an iron brace. The black reared back and shied away. He galloped to the far end of the corral and stood wild-eyed and nervous.

"It was a good idea, but it didn't work," Jerry grunted ruefully. "I hate to do it, Pete; but the only way I can see we'll ever get him home is to have one of the boys here rope him, throw him, put on a halter, and cross-tie him. We may be able to put a rope against his rump, then, and force him in; but it will take at least two men, one of them an experienced roper, to do it. You stay here. I'll see what I can do."

He started toward the lower end of the yard, but a sudden cry from Peter stopped him.

"No! Please! He's had enough. I don't want to start manhandling him when he's just beginning to think maybe there's one person in the world who isn't his enemy."

Jerry leaned against the fence and scratched his head. "You're right, but what in Sam Hill can we do? We can't leave him here forever. You can't come way out here and halter-break him. They're cramped for room whenever there's a big shipment of cattle in, and they're not going to let His Nibs occupy one whole corral by himself."

"O.K.," Peter agreed reluctantly. "Get help; but let's try to figure out some other way to do it, when they get here."

When he was out of sight, Peter spoke to the black pleadingly. "Look, boy, what we're trying to do is for your own good. At our place there's a nice stall, a soft bed of straw, and good hay and oats waiting for you. Come on! Trust us a little." Peter got out the oats and again scattered them on the ground right into the trailer.

The black cocked his ears forward, watching and listening. He gazed at Peter without hostility, but he made no move toward the trailer. Jerry returned with two helpers; the black galloped to the far end of the corral, and Peter watched in dismay as one of them tossed a loop skillfully over the neck of the running horse and snubbed him to one of the heavy posts. Another loop, tied on the opposite side, left the black powerless to do more than rear and plunge.

Peter watched the ropes cut into the black's hide as he struggled uselessly against them. He started to yell "Take 'em off," but suddenly the horse realized he was trapped. He stopped struggling and stood with legs wide apart, eyes flashing and nostrils flaring. Jerry and Peter talked fast and hard to keep the two yardmen from throwing him, blindfolding him, and putting on a halter. Peter begged to try it in his own way first, and they finally gave in—after repeated warnings to keep out of the way of the colt's hoofs and teeth.

"Go outside, all of you," Peter begged.

He advanced to within a few feet of the black's head, just out of the danger range, talking all the way, using the same quiet, soothing tone that had been effective before. The colt pulled back at first, straining at the ropes; but he made no move to bite or strike out. Peter finally reached his withers and put a tentative hand on his neck. The black trembled but stood firm. Peter stroked him gently, talking on and on in that same low tone. In a few minutes the trembling stopped. Four or five times the boy backed off and then walked up to the colt's head unhesitatingly, putting out his hand each time. Slowly he reached farther and farther along the neck until he was touching the head between the eyes . . . coming down the face toward the nose. Unable to believe his good fortune, Peter finally went over and asked for the halter.

"I'll try it," he told Jerry. "If he's terribly afraid of it, I won't force him."

"You're doing O.K.," Jerry said approvingly. "Wish your Dad could see you. There's no bad streak in that horse or he'd never have tamed down this much. He's scared, but he's basically sensible. I think you two will get along, even though you've never broken a horse from scratch. He's not like the usual bronc in any sense of the word."

After another fifteen minutes of careful approach, while the yard hands watched wonderingly, Peter had the halter buckled on the black's head. A rope was tied to the ring and brought forward to the manger of the trailer. It was put through a hole in the front and Jerry wrapped it around the rear bumper of the car.

"We'll have to cast off the side ropes," he told Peter. "Can't have him pull them into the trailer and choke himself or get all mixed up in them. Besides, the fellows want their ropes back. Can you get them off?"

"I can try," Peter said.

He knew the only way he could do it was to loosen them from the posts, then slip each one back through the loop; for they couldn't be taken off over the halter without unfastening the rope leading to the trailer. It was a tedious job; for as soon as he no longer felt the pull of the side ropes, the colt tried to get away again. Finally he realized that, although he could now move in a narrow arc, the front rope pulled relentlessly toward the trailer, and that all his rearing and pulling back were useless.

"Learns fast," Jerry commented. "Shows he's smart."

When the black had quieted down again, Peter worked the ropes off of him one at a time. The two helpers came up and brought a rope gently across his hindquarters, each one holding an end. Feeling the touch of it, the black lunged forward toward the trailer and Jerry pulled up the slack, snubbing him just that much closer to it. A few feet at a time they worked him forward until, with a final lunge, he was up and in the trailer. They pulled the rope tight, tied him to the manger, flung up the tail gate quickly—and the job was done.

It was a good thing the end gate was heavy and well reinforced with iron; for as soon as he realized he was trapped, the colt's hind legs crashed against it like twin battering rams. Finding it unyielding, he lapsed finally into an occasional sharp kick that served only to shake the trailer and worry Peter.

"Come on," Jerry said. "Let's get going quick, before he thinks up some more devilment."

Peter jumped into the car beside Jerry and they started off slowly. He heaved a sigh of relief, but already he was worrying about how to get the black unloaded and into his stall without mishap.

CHAPTER III

Problem Horse

There were frequent sharp crashes from the trailer. When Jerry finally drew up at the door of the Riding Academy, he let out a sigh of relief.

"Well, at least he's here. Ask your Dad where to put him. I'm beginning to wonder if I was so smart to think of this after all. Better get both the stablemen too. We'll need 'em."

With some trepidation Peter sought out his father, who was busy and beset with many problems. He would not appreciate having the Saturday routine disrupted. Peter was lucky enough to find him at the house having a few minutes of stolen relaxation.

John Morgan smiled when Peter explained the predicament, but his voice was firm. "All right, we'll help. Put your colt in the outside shed. We're crowded inside and, since he's not used to being penned up, he'd probably raise a fuss and upset all the other horses. Out there he probably won't be quite such a nuisance. But remember you're to take no chances handling him till I'm satisfied he's not dangerous. Can't imagine how Jerry could think any scrubby broomtail from a wild herd would ever make a really good horse anyway."

He rose and followed Peter outside. Jerry had already found the stablemen. They opened the stall door; Jerry backed the trailer tight up to the opening and let the tail gate down into the stall itself. Charcoal plunged down and huddled against the far wall, trembling but defiant. The men slammed the door shut before he could make a move. The colt was safe inside the stall, but neither John Morgan nor the two stablemen had caught more than a glimpse of him. Peter had noted with dismay that the stall had a dirt floor; was narrow and dark and at the very end of the shed, farthest from the hay and grain supply. No chance to keep a supply of feed in the other empty stall either, because of the rats and mice.

Expecting to hear plenty of commotion, Peter waited; but there was no sound at all. Surprised, he cautiously opened the upper half of the Dutch door a few inches and peered into the gloom. The colt still stood against the farther wall, trembling. Apparently he had used up all his surplus energy kicking at the tail gate. Peter turned, to find his father at his shoulder.

"How about a look at him?" John Morgan opened the door a little wider. Peter watched anxiously. "Well." His father's voice betrayed doubt and a trace of amusement. "He's rough and rangy . . . better than

[37]

some broomtails though. But I'm willing to be shown.
We won't turn any of the other horses out into this
lot, and you can work with him here, Pete. Don't go
into the stall yet. One of the boys can feed and water
him through the top of the door for a few days. Then
you can take over. In the meantime let him be quiet
and alone. Maybe it will calm him down. We'll look
him over together out in the lot in a day or two."

Peter was itching to get his hands on the colt again,
but he knew better than to argue. He didn't like the
way his father used that term "broomtail" in derision.
It was different when Jerry said it, half jokingly. He
wondered how his mother would like the colt. He
started eagerly toward the house to get her, then remembered his father's orders to stay away. He limped
slowly and reluctantly toward the main stable, but
stopped when he heard a crash of hoofs against the
wooden planks behind him. Charcoal must have re-
gained his energy. Peter didn't blame him for hating
the small, dingy stall after the freedom of the open
plains. He listened, but there was no further sound;
so he went on.

"Look here," John Morgan said as he entered the
Academy office. "Don't forget Star in your excitement
over the new horse. Star's still your responsibility to
feed, exercise, and love. The stable helpers have more
to do than they should; but now that you'll be taking
on regular duties around here, it will be a help."

Peter knew that was meant as a gentle reminder of his promises. His father needn't worry; he'd do his part. But taking care of Star, helping in the stable, and keeping up his studies when school started in a few weeks—how would he ever have any time left to work with Charcoal? Peter went to bed wondering about a dozen things, one of them being how soon he would hear from Dodo and what she would have to say about the new horse. Peter thought of Dodo as he had last seen her—pert, freckle-faced, redheaded, just a year younger than he, full of the old Nick but as good-hearted as they come. They had ridden a lot together those last few years when John Morgan worked for Dodo's father. They had scrapped and made up a hundred times; but Dodo knew horses and how to handle them, and Peter respected her for it.

Early Sunday morning the Morgan family was awakened by a loud knocking. Peter, half asleep, heard his father go to the door. Then he dimly heard the words "the boy's colt," and he snapped into sudden wakefulness. It was Bob, the head stableman.

"Yep," the stocky little Scot was saying, "kicked that stall almost to pieces, he did. Found out when we came to feed him at five. If he can do all that without shoes, what'll he do when he's shod?"

"Did he get out?" Mr. Morgan demanded impatiently.

"Darn near it! He kicked half the wall out between him and the next stall, and most of the lower half of the back door out to the lot. What now, boss?"

Peter jumped out of bed and limped into the living room. His hip caught with a sharp twinge of pain, but he was too excited to be concerned.

"Is Charcoal hurt?" he demanded anxiously.

Bob smiled. "Nothing but a little skin off one leg. Matches the rope burn on his neck. I was just askin' your Dad here . . . what do we do with him now?"

"How high is that fence around the lot?" John Morgan asked. "About five feet?"

"Yep." Bob scratched his head. "It has good strong poles too. Reckon those ought to hold him."

"Turn him in there, then. Better keep an eye on him till Peter gets dressed. He might even try to kick that fence down."

Peter saw that his father was worried and annoyed but not really angry. He dressed silently and hurried to the outside shed. To Peter, Charcoal looked handsomer than ever. Turning wide, innocent eyes on his master, he showed no fear at his approach. Glad that the hands-off command had apparently been lifted, Peter tried to walk right up to the colt. The yard was much larger than the corral at the packing plant. Charcoal was feeling his freedom. He let the boy come within ten feet; then with a devilish gleam in his eye he kicked up his heels and galloped madly to the opposite side. There was a little grass growing up along the fence and he fell to cropping that, keeping his eye on Peter all the while. He seemed satisfied for the present and made no effort to get out of the enclosure.

Peter sat on a box by the fence and watched the black with pride. He might be a problem, but he was certainly an interesting one. Bob came with hay and some oats in a pan and set them down inside the fence. The colt advanced cautiously and began eating. Not more than fifty feet away, Peter sat quietly until his mother called him in to breakfast.

"How's he doing?" John Morgan asked when Peter sat down at the table.

Peter looked sheepish. "O.K. He hasn't tried to kick anything yet, and he's eating peacefully. Once he let me come almost up to him."

"Who's going to fix that stall?" His father sounded upset. "It'll take heavy two-by-sixes or two-by-eights to wall him up, and they cost money."

"I will," Peter promised. "And I'll pay for the new boards if you'll just give me time. I've been thinking maybe I could get Hank Elkins' paper route. He's tired of it. I'd have to get up awfully early; but I'd have a little time left to work with Charcoal mornings, even after school starts. I could still do the barn chores afternoons, and study at night. That way I could earn enough to pay back the thirty dollars Charcoal cost, and for part of his feed too. Maybe I wouldn't have to work quite so long in the afternoons and I could train Charcoal then too. Two lessons a day ought to get him gentle in no time."

John Morgan pushed back his chair and smiled at his son. "Got it all figured out, haven't you? Only rub is that, with that bad hip of yours, I know Doc Bush would think you still weren't up to that long paper route on foot every morning. Riding a bicycle would be even harder. The doctor cautioned you especially against that. Maybe you figured on using a helicopter."

"I can ride Star," Peter told him eagerly. "I went over the route with Hank once in his Dad's car. It's mostly putting the paper in rural boxes. Once the pack of papers is tied on my saddle, I'd be at just the right height to reach the boxes. What few places get it direct . . . I could throw the rolled-up paper easy from the road onto the porch. Hank does it from his bike. Please, Dad, I'd like to try it."

"What do you think, Elizabeth?" John Morgan turned to his wife, whose dubious expression he had been watching.

"Well, Peter's pretty loaded down as it is. Every time he's overdone in the past, it seemed to make his hip and back worse. I'd say yes only if we call Dr. Bush long distance and get his approval."

"Good idea." John Morgan turned to Peter. "Now, son, don't get your hopes too high. I doubt whether this wild broomtail from the hills is worth all the trouble you're taking with him."

"He'll turn out. You'll see." Peter spoke almost

fiercely. "As for Doc Bush . . . he'll say it's O.K. if you tell him I'll be happy doing it."

The Morgans had never ceased to rely on the advice of the good country doctor who had pulled Peter through the anxious months following the accident, and they had made several trips back to Glen Valley so he could check up on Peter's condition.

"We'll call him tonight," John Morgan promised. "More likely to catch him in. In the meantime you'd better find out from the paper if you can really have the job. No use wasting money on a call if they wouldn't hire you."

Peter had to be content with that. After breakfast he hurried back to the corral, carrying a good stout lead rope. Charcoal still wore the halter with a fragment of rope hanging to it. Sometime before the day was over he hoped to get a lead rope on the colt.

All morning Peter patiently sat in the lot. He set a tiny pan of oats beside him on the ground, knowing the black couldn't help smelling them if he came anywhere near. But it was nearly noon before Charcoal grabbed a mouthful of oats and veered hastily away. Several times he repeated the performance, but Peter sat tight. The last time, Charcoal stood looking at him a moment before he moved away. Peter hated the feeling of inactivity and the long waiting, but he knew it was the only way to keep from losing all the ground he had gained. He remembered the hours he had spent wooing Star, and how it had paid in the end.

Now, after the trailer trip, he had to win the black's confidence all over again.

Right after lunch Peter called Hank Elkins and asked to be recommended to the newspaper's circulation manager. An hour later the man called to say the job was Peter's any time he wanted to take over. Lightheartedly Peter cleaned his allotted number of stalls, hoping desperately that Dr. Bush would agree. Then he started back to Charcoal.

By now, Sunday riding parties were beginning to pass the lot. One of the main trails followed the enclosure for several hundred feet before taking off through the woods. When he came in sight of the lot, Peter stopped short. There was Charcoal galloping wildly along the fence, whinnying in high, piercing tones, crouching and sizing up the bars as if he had half a notion to jump them. Peter was plain scared. As soon as the horses were out of sight, the black settled down to an aimless circling of the lot; but each time a rider or group of riders appeared, the same thing happened all over again.

Sometimes the horses outside, as if in answer to the colt's shrill summons, became excited and gave their riders some trouble. The mares especially were affected by the young stallion's trumpeting calls. Here was another serious problem. Charcoal was somewhere around three. He would have to be gelded, and that would be another expense.

Momentarily discouraged, Peter cupped his chin in

his hands and, with elbows on knees, stared moodily across the lot at the temporarily calm Charcoal. Riders who knew the boy strolled over, after they had turned in their horses, to find out what it was all about. Already word of the "wild broomtail from the Horse Heaven country" had spread through the whole Academy, and everyone wanted to see him.

Peter wished they wouldn't come yet—just when he was trying to get Charcoal quieted down and accustomed to his new surroundings. He had to go outside the lot to keep people from coming in, so the afternoon was well-nigh wasted. By four o'clock he knew there would be trouble unless something was done about the fence. And of course his father had to come over to check just as an especially large group of riders went by and Charcoal practically climbed the rails.

"Look here!" John Morgan sounded more than annoyed this time. "We can't have your horse acting like that. With the rent horses getting upset we could have an accident, and that's always bad publicity for a riding stable. Besides, Charcoal acts as if he'd like to go over that fence any minute—high as it is. Of course he couldn't jump five feet; but he could crash the top rail and maybe get over it somehow, or hurt himself trying.

"There's only one solution—the fence will have to be built up another rail in height, and that, my boy, takes time and money." His voice grew grim. "Pete,

I'll do that one more thing for you because your heart seems so set on this black bronc. And then there will be the gelding to pay for when a veterinary can get anywhere near him. Hope you get your job all right, or I'll go broke supporting him."

Fortunately there were extra poles on the place, bought with the intention of enclosing another exercise lot when time permitted. "We'll just have to use them for this," John Morgan said. "All twenty dollars' worth of them."

As soon as the horses were fed for the evening, one stableman was left to take care of the incoming riders while a crew of six—consisting of Bob, a young man volunteer who boarded his horse at the stable, Jerry, Hank Elkins, John Morgan, and Peter—got together and raised the height of the fence to nearly six feet.

"Sure glad we didn't cut off those posts when we first built this," John Morgan said, wiping the sweat from his forehead as he finished driving the last nail. "Glad you two happened along at just the right time too." He nodded to Hank and Jerry.

They'd all made a lark of it and, with so many, the work had gone fast. They finished just before dark. As he walked over to the house beside his father, Peter's voice grew gruff with embarrassment.

"Gee, Dad, thanks for being so patient. I promise you won't be sorry."

John Morgan smiled in the gathering dusk and laid a hand momentarily on Peter's arm. "It's all right, son.

I think we've got the situation under control at last. We still have to see how your colt responds to his gentling, but I can't help feeling that you're wasting your time. He's an unknown quantity, Peter."

When Dr. Bush suggested that they let him try the paper route and see how it went, Peter was in seventh heaven.

"The swell part of it," he told his father, "is that I'll be giving Star his daily exercise at the same time I do my route, and that's time saved right there."

"You have a point," John Morgan agreed, "but remember it's just a trial. If you show any signs of wear and tear, either your paper route or the colt must go—maybe both."

Peter was pleased as punch to get a letter from Dodo a few days later. It was short and to the point: "The new horse sounds swell. When do I get to see him?"

Peter meant to answer; but he wasn't much on letter writing, and there was so much to do that he kept putting it off. Anyway he didn't know how to answer Dodo's question, for Glen Valley lay one hundred and fifty miles to the south.

CHAPTER IV

Charcoal Decides His Own Future

During the rest of the summer vacation Peter worked hard to win the affection of the black colt. Slowly he gained ground, spending a full hour with Charcoal in the morning and another in the afternoon. Besides that, whenever all his work was done, he just sat in the shade of a big tree in one corner of the lot, watching the black's every move.

At the end of the second week Charcoal would let Peter approach, rub his neck or forehead, and feed him wisps of grass. By the end of the third week he would follow when led, and it was a proud moment for Peter when midway of the fourth week the wild colt lifted his head and nickered softly at sight of him.

Hank Elkins, who liked to come by and idle away the long August afternoons, often sat with Peter, watching the colt; but he knew very little about horses and had no particular desire to help. Many of the riders stopped to chat or check on Charcoal's progress, but most of them showed a tolerant amusement and expressed the opinion that Peter was simply wasting his time.

There was the day Connie Pearson came along and wanted Peter to ride with her. She was one of his Dad's best customers; so he hardly dared refuse, although Connie and all of her crowd bored him to death.

All during the ride he talked about Charcoal. "You ought to understand why I'm so crazy about him," he told her. "You say you can tell a good horse when you see him, any time."

"Sure I like good horses." Connie tossed her black hair back out of her eyes as they dismounted. "But I also like company that at least knows I exist. All you think about is that black colt." She stalked away in disgust.

Bewildered at her annoyance, Peter walked slowly back to Charcoal. Maybe he shouldn't spend so much time with the black, but it was the first time he had had a horse to train himself, from the very beginning. Anyway girls were funny about some things. The love of training was in his blood; and this was one way he could satisfy it, even though his life ambition was to be a commercial artist.

Peter stood and waited for the colt to circle and come up to him. "Look, boy, they just don't understand how important you are. However you turn out, it'll be *my* doing. Nobody's handing you to me all finished and ready to show, the way Star was. You'll never take Star's place; but you're no ordinary broom-tail, no ordinary wild bronc, and we'll prove it to everybody . . . someday."

When school started, Peter had to cut down on the training periods; but by that time Charcoal was following him around like a dog. One day he laid a saddle blanket gently on the colt's back. Charcoal promptly bucked it off. Peter patiently picked it up and replaced it. Twice more the colt got rid of it; the fourth time he looked around at it resignedly and let it stay. Now it was only a step to fastening it on loosely with a wide canvas girth. Each day Peter drew the girth a little tighter and let the colt wear it awhile. Once or twice Charcoal tried to roll it off; but, finding that did no good, he accepted the girth as he had the blanket.

"One of these days," Peter told his father, "I'll put a light English saddle over the blanket. I think he'll stand for it now."

"Well, maybe," John Morgan agreed cautiously. "But, mind you, I don't want him rolling on one of our good English saddles and breaking the tree. Take it easy, son. Remember you're not to be the first one to get on him when the time comes. No taking chances with that game hip of yours. Those are orders!"

"Yes, sir!" Peter said. When his father used that tone of voice, you didn't argue back. But inwardly he rebelled. Why couldn't he have the satisfaction of being the first to actually ride the horse he'd worked with so long? He was sure he could stick on, and anyway Charcoal probably wouldn't make a bit of fuss.

All that fall and winter, things went along so well that Peter could hardly believe his good fortune. He enjoyed the early-morning paper route, and the boy and his beautiful black Walking Horse became such favorites with the subscribers that it was hard for Peter to make his rounds in the allotted time. There were almost always one or two early risers out to greet him and visit a little as they took the paper from him personally. The word was passed along, and before he knew it he had a dozen new subscribers. He was glad to get them, but the route took more time and encroached on Charcoal's morning training hour. Just the same, he couldn't very well turn down business and expect to hold his job.

One day John Morgan surprised his son with a very simple question. "What kind of horse are you trying to make out of Charcoal? Straight all-round pleasure animal, stock horse for western or reining classes, three-gaited, five-gaited, fine harness, or jumper?"

Peter stopped short in his progress toward the kitchen. Suddenly he realized he didn't know. "To tell you the truth, Dad, I hadn't thought about that. So far he hasn't shown any natural tendency to gait. I guess I'll make him an all-round pleasure horse. He's not the type for western classes, in spite of his background—too much of the Thoroughbred look about him. Gosh, he might even turn out to be a runner!"

"He might," John Morgan said dryly, "but not as a product of Morgan and Son. I haven't the time, money, or inclination to sponsor a race horse. Better forget that one."

Walking out to the corral, Peter realized it was high time he decided just what he *was* training Charcoal for. The colt just couldn't be allowed to develop any-which-way like Topsy. There ought to be some sort of plan. But what? The question was answered for all of them in mid-April.

It was one of those cooler spring days when the tang of frost is still in the air, setting a person's blood to racing and raising a horse's spirits to a new high. Peter felt full of the joy of living, and Charcoal raced around the corral kicking up his heels and buck-jumping with delight when the time for the morning lesson arrived. The boy had all he could do to talk the black into keeping all four feet on the ground at the same time.

"We'd better cut down on your daily supply of oats," he admonished reprovingly as he bridled him and snapped the reins into rings on the surcingle.

Each day, now, he did that for half an hour or so, accustoming Charcoal to the feel of the bit, teaching him to arch and supple his neck. The lesson finally concluded, Peter had breakfast and went off to school.

It was just like any other morning in the big gray building that was West Hills Junior High—at least until nearly noon, when the principal came into the study hall and motioned Peter into the hall.

"Your mother wants you on the phone," he said.

Peter paled. He knew the folks wouldn't call him at school unless there was something really wrong. Maybe his father had been hurt. There was always a chance, for some of the horses he trained were a handful even for a skilled trainer. Peter felt his knees turn to rubber as he picked up the receiver. If it wasn't his father, it might be his mother; or it might be Charcoal. The colt could be sick or injured.

"Peter," his mother said without preamble, "Charcoal's gone. You'd better come right home and help look for him. I've asked the principal to excuse you."

"Gone?" Peter sounded both relieved and amazed. "How do you mean . . . gone? Did somebody leave the gate open?"

"No." Mrs. Morgan's voice revealed her wonderment. "He jumped. Left some of his hairs and a little hide on the top rail. Your Dad and two of the men are out hunting him. I'll tell you the rest when you get here. If they locate him, they may need your help in catching him."

Peter was lucky enough to board a bus just outside the building. Back at the Academy, he quickly changed into a pair of jeans and jumped into the family car with his mother. The men had taken the station wagon, and John Morgan was on horseback.

"Your Dad's worried sick," Mrs. Morgan said as they pulled out of the yard and started up one of the many gravel roads that wound around among the hills. "You know this neighborhood is fast becoming an exclusive residential section and there have been several complaints about having a riding academy here. Only because the stable was here first, and because we keep it so clean and sanitary, have the authorities refrained from making trouble. You know that freedom is very likely to go to Charcoal's head, and he could do a lot of damage to expensive lawns and gardens. Let's hope he's found . . . soon."

Peter swallowed hard and stared straight ahead. Couldn't Mom see that he was worried too and quit rubbing it in? He knew all about the complaints, but he knew they'd never be shut down so long as the place was kept clean.

"Don't worry, we'll find him. Dad's probably following his tracks right now, better than we could in a car. What I can't figure out is how he ever got over that fence. Jeepers, Mom, do you realize what that means—clearing nearly six feet of solid fence, even with a long take-off? Charcoal's a natural at jumping, Mom. That's what we'll make of him—a jumper."

Mrs. Morgan's voice was sharp. "Maybe so, maybe so, but *you'll* do no jumping on him. If he's trained as a jumper, somebody else will have to do it."

Peter's face fell. He hadn't considered that angle

of it, but he knew she was right. Moreover, even if he were able to school and ride a jumper, he didn't know how. Handling jumping horses required a special technique, and his father left the handling of the many jumpers at the Academy to a young assistant, Dick Stearns, who specialized in just that.

For three hours Mrs. Morgan and Peter scoured the roads in the West Hills section, but saw no sign of Charcoal. Once they saw the station wagon and flagged it down, only to find that Bob and Dick had had no better luck. At dinner time a weary quintet assembled back at the Academy. No one, not even John Morgan, had word of the missing black.

"Must have taken off for the hills of home," Bob said laconically. "He'd have kind of a hard time swimming the Columbia River though."

"We might as well fix supper and eat," Mrs. Morgan said. "Worrying won't get us anywhere. Surely we'll hear something sooner or later."

"Anyone finding him won't know where he came from," Peter reminded them disconsolately. "After all he wasn't wearing a collar and tag."

Dinner over, they sat glumly in the living room till Mr. Morgan had to go out to an evening riding class for business women, whom he instructed in the inside ring. Peter wandered around the house like a lost sheep, staring out the window toward the empty lot, imagining all sorts of fatalities for Charcoal.

"Peter!"

It was his mother's voice, calling excitedly from the living room. Peter hurried in to find her listening intently to the radio. She put her finger on her lips as he started to speak. It was the local newscaster from a downtown studio.

"A humorous note was injected into the day's routine for local police when they were called to the West Hills section early this afternoon to pick up a loose horse which had done extensive damage to lawns and gardens in three exclusive homes, tied up traffic on a busy highway, and scared three helpless housewives half to death. It took an entire squad of policemen, including three motorcycle cops, plus two Humane Society officers, to finally corner the animal in a fenced back yard, rope it, and transport it to the Humane Society barns in a truck. Here the horse is proving an even greater problem, as he seems to be allergic to stalls. A frenzied plea is being sent out by the Humane Society to the owner to please come and claim said beast at once. He is a black stallion with a white blaze, judged to be about three or four years old. Unless called for promptly, the horse will have to be destroyed without the usual waiting period."

"Charcoal!" Peter gasped. He looked at his mother in dismay.

"Yes," she said. "And I suppose by tomorrow they'll announce the owner, and that will be undesirable publicity for the West Hills Riding Academy." She sighed. "Well, I'll call the Humane Society right away and tell them we're coming. You'd better go break the news to your Dad. Somebody will have to take the trailer and go after Charcoal."

Peter sought out his father, but it took a lot of courage to interrupt the lesson this time. John Morgan was upset, and Peter didn't blame him.

"Go get Bob and Dick Stearns, and take the closed trailer." he snapped. "Probably take all three of you to get him into it. When you're back, we'll tie that darned broomtail down with chains."

"But, Dad," Peter interrupted, "think what he did! He jumped nearly six feet."

"I don't care if he jumped sixty feet," John Morgan said tersely. "There'll be the devil to pay tomorrow when those homeowners get on our trail. As for the horse's future . . . he's cooked his goose now as far as I'm concerned. Well, quit standing there and go get him. We'll talk about the rest of it tomorrow."

CHAPTER V

First Ride

Getting Charcoal into the trailer was not quite so hard this time, but it took all of Peter's persuasion and a good big pan of oats to do it. At the Academy they put him back in the stall until the fence could be built even higher. Peter was too worried to think very clearly. He had just finished saving enough to pay for the reinforcing of the stall and the cost of the poles to build up the fence the first time. The rest of his money had gone into feed and incidentals, so as yet he hadn't been able to pay back Charcoal's purchase price.

Technically the colt still belonged to John Morgan, and he could do as he liked with him. Peter had to admit the black's latest escapade would have tried the patience of a saint. He'd never be able to catch up with the expenses. He didn't dare think what bills might be presented by irate homeowners whose yards and gardens had suffered.

Not only would Charcoal soon have to be gelded

but he was about ready for his first shoeing. For the first time, lack of money loomed as a very big problem to Peter. Sudden doubt swept over him as the men shut the colt in the reinforced stall, and he heard two or three tentative kicks. Had he taken on a bigger job than he could handle? He waited to see what would happen. But, apparently finding the heavy planks too much for his unshod hoofs, Charcoal settled down. Peter mulled over his father's threat as he walked slowly to the house. He just *couldn't* let Charcoal go now. The colt trusted him and was about ready for the final test—a rider on his back.

It was a sober father and son who sat alone at the breakfast table the next morning, the dishes cleared away and Mrs. Morgan busy in the kitchen washing them.

"I lay awake a long time last night thinking about your horse, son. I was going to tell you this morning he'd simply have to go, that keeping a wild, free thing like him here in a city riding academy is absolutely impractical. Then I called Jerry, wondering if he could offer a solution, hoping maybe he'd keep him out there for you. For some strange reason Jerry shares your faith in the horse. He could hardly believe he'd made that amazing jump. He wants to pay any reasonable claims that may arise out of yesterday's escapade, but I couldn't let him do that except on a loan basis. He has an old electric fence he isn't using; and he'll string it up around Charcoal's lot to keep him in, if I'll just consent to let him stay. What could I say in the face of all that?

"We'll have to nail short extensions on all the fence posts, and put on a double strand of the wire; but Jerry says if you'll help he'll put it up for us."

Peter started to speak, but his father silenced him with a wave of the hand. "Jerry went on to say that Charcoal's future is clear. He must be trained as a jumper. I don't know just how, since you mustn't try riding a jumper yourself; it's not my line, and I can't spare Dick to help you. If you can work it out somehow, it's O.K. with me. The horse hasn't a mean streak in him, I'm sure. He's just young and full of life, and he has a wild horse's natural hatred of confinement; but, so far, it all adds up to a big headache. You'd better call Jerry and thank him. He says when you don't need the electric fence equipment any longer he wants it back."

Peter not only called Jerry but was at his elbow every minute, helping to rig up the electric fence the next day. When they had finished and the black was once more out in the open lot, Jerry surveyed him thoughtfully.

"It's just about time to try riding him. One of these days I'll have a go at it."

Jerry drove off. Peter stood a moment thinking. His heart was pounding in his chest and he felt very daring. With sudden resolve he went and got his saddle and bridle. He tied the black to the fence and slipped on the bridle slowly and carefully. He started to put on the saddle, then stopped. Maybe it would be better bareback the first time. He laid the saddle aside and surveyed Charcoal speculatively. Would he show the results of these many long months of patient handling, the slow build-up to this moment? Or would he forget everything and revert to the wild in his shock at finding someone on his back?

Peter didn't hurry. He stood patting Charcoal on the neck, rubbing him between the ears and up under the mane where the dandruff collected. He led him over to a box in the corner of the yard and stood on it, leaning against the colt's back. At first Charcoal moved away restlessly, not liking the pressure; then, after Peter had repeated it several times, he stood firm, tolerating it. Suddenly Peter slipped a leg over his back and sat quietly, grasping his mane.

Charcoal turned his head and looked at him in surprise. He took a few tentative steps, humped his back, took a couple of mild crowhops, and then decided against any show of violence. Peter clucked to him softly, and he moved off uncertainly at a walk. By the time they had circled the yard a couple of times Charcoal was walking as calmly as if he'd always been used to a rider. He made very little more fuss when Peter put on the saddle and rode again. He took a few side steps, pranced, threw his head a time or two . . . and that was all. Peter tried to guide him with the reins, but the black was awkward and unaware of what was expected of him.

Because he couldn't twist his body or bear his full weight on the bad leg, Peter had to steady himself with the handhold when Charcoal began to trot. He eased the black down to a walk again. Gradually Charcoal relaxed and stepped out lightly with a springiness that was a pleasure to feel. After a few rounds of the lot, Peter slid off slowly, so as not to startle him, and removed the saddle. He was bursting with happiness, but he couldn't figure out how he was going to explain to his Dad what he had done. His first thought was to get him right away, confess, and then show him how beautifully Charcoal was behaving. But no, better to wait a couple of days more, so there would be no possible slip-up, and let Charcoal learn to respond better to the reins.

Peter waited his chance at the phone alone, called up Jerry, told him the news, and asked him to come try the colt as soon as possible. He was still tingling from the thrill of that first ride.

"Your Dad's going to be mad," Jerry said, startled. "You should have kept your word, Pete, but I can understand how you felt. I'll come over and try him tomorrow."

True to his word, Jerry turned up and rode the next day. He moved slowly and was very gentle, so that Charcoal behaved almost as well as with Peter. He did so well, in fact, that Peter couldn't resist showing him off to his father. The latter nodded approvingly when he saw the colt in action.

"Glad you had sense enough to let Jerry ride him first," he said.

Peter looked sheepish. "I'm afraid I didn't." He expected to be scolded, but he was not prepared for the hard anger in his father's voice.

"I've treated you right on this wild-bronc proposition. In the face of what I told you, the least you could have done was ask me before you rode him." John Morgan turned on his heel.

Peter opened his mouth to defend himself, then shut it again and watched bitterly as his father walked away. He knew he had done wrong, but he had been afraid to ask. Somehow his father had been different since they had the Academy—so much more irritable, so much harder to talk things over with.

Jerry came again the next day. "After all, I got you into this in the first place," he said. He got a long rope and together he and Peter set up some low jumps in the lot.

"You'll need a long whip," Jerry explained. "You don't hit him with it, of course, but you crack it to keep him on the course. And don't rush him, son. Too many promising jumpers are ruined by making them jump too high when young. He shouldn't be jumping regularly more than three or three and a half feet until he's between four and five; then work up the height gradually. A good jumper usually comes into his own at about six or so and keeps at it for years."

"I'll remember." Already Peter was planning ahead. Even if Dick, the assistant riding master who had trained and jumped show horses all his life, didn't have the time to help him, there was no reason why he couldn't watch and learn while Dick trained other people's horses.

For several weeks Peter haunted Dick whenever the latter was exercising a jumper. He and his father spoke only when necessary, and there was a sense of strain all the time when they were in the house together. Consequently he avoided his father whenever he could. Then one day Dick offered to help with Charcoal after his duties at the Academy were over. Peter's father grunted when he heard about it; but he raised no objections, saying that if Dick wanted to make a postman's holiday out of his off hours it was his own affair.

Peter had already taught Charcoal how to longe or circle at the end of the long line. Now Dick put the low jumps in place—two pole barriers and a brush jump—and sent him over the course without a rider. Wide wings at the jumps and the figure of Dick flourishing the whip made the black take the first jump easily. After trying to run around the edge a time or two and having the whip cracked almost at his hindquarters, Charcoal settled down to business. In fact, he took the jumps with so much to spare that Peter wanted to raise them.

"Nope," Dick insisted. "Don't rush him. The way to build bone, stamina, and good strong hindquarters in a jumper is to take it slow and easy. But he'll have to be shod before you can train him like this regularly. It's too hard on his hoofs and pasterns otherwise."

Peter had been putting off the shoeing, knowing it might be an ordeal for everybody concerned. Now he dropped everything else for a whole week and concentrated on handling the colt's feet and legs. Every day he picked up first one hoof and then the other, rubbing the glossy black legs, cleaning out the hoofs, rewarding Charcoal with a carrot or a lump of sugar when he no longer pulled away. At the end of the week he felt it was fairly safe to call the blacksmith, a big, husky Swede, slow-moving and kind. There would be no trouble now, Peter thought—and he was right.

Peter was riding Charcoal slowly around the big indoor ring, teaching him to respond to the bit, the day Connie Pearson and he had their memorable fight. She had finished her ride and, passing the open door of the big ring, caught sight of him.

"Hi, Peter. Mind if I watch?"

"No, of course not."

Secretly Peter was a little flattered at having an audience. At first everyone had been tremendously interested in the black colt. Now he was an old story, and few of the stable's customers lingered to watch or ask questions. Peter held the reins just a shade tighter, collecting Charcoal up to the bit. He couldn't resist making him arch his neck and show off a little.

The black, now in his fourth year, had developed wonderfully. The gangly, coltish look was gone. He still had the long, rangy lines of a Thoroughbred; but they were well-turned lines, minus the awkwardness and indeterminate gait. With early spring in the air the thick winter coat, just beginning to shed out, had a sheen to it very different from the ragged unkempt coat he bore when Peter first glimpsed him. Connie had not seen Charcoal for quite a while. She watched with slowly widening eyes.

"Hey! He's a beauty! Hear you're going to make a jumper out of him. That's my specialty. How about a ride?"

Peter swallowed nervously. He pretended he didn't hear, but when Connie yelled at him again, the second time around, he couldn't ignore her. He turned Charcoal toward her and pulled him to a stop.

"Look, Connie. Maybe later you can ride him, but he's young and green. No one but Jerry and me has ever been on him. Not even Dad. He's hardly bridle-wise yet."

"Listen here, Peter Morgan! I know a lot more about jumping than you do. You've never ridden over a real jump in your life. All I want to do is ride him around the ring. He's perfectly quiet. You know very well I can ride anything you can."

Peter stared at her angrily. He had spent eight careful months with Charcoal, bringing him along step by step, never inciting him to rebellion. Connie meant well enough; but she was heavy-handed, showed poor judgment at times, and often lost her temper if a horse acted up.

"Connie, I'm not letting you ride him now. Maybe this summer—"

"All right for you, Peter. I don't have to come to your old Academy. There's two in this town. And I'll get my friends to go to the other one too."

Turning, Connie flounced out the door.

"Spoiled brat!" Peter muttered between his teeth.

He tried to go on with his ride, but he couldn't keep his mind on what he was doing. Connie meant what she said. He knew it by the angry gleam in her eyes, and from her actions in the past. Even though he wouldn't miss her or her friends either, he knew his father could ill afford to lose them as customers.

CHAPTER VI

Danger Ahead

As Peter had feared, there was an aftermath to the Pearson affair. That evening at dinner his father inquired gravely, "What happened today between you and Connie Pearson? She slapped down her riding ticket, asked for a refund, and marched out in a huff. Said it was all on account of you, but she was out the door before I could get the details."

Peter confessed. "I'm sorry, Dad, but what else could I do? Charcoal's high-strung and only half-trained. Connie's hard on any horse. She might have been hurt."

John Morgan nodded, but he looked far from happy. "Seems as if every time there's trouble around here that Charcoal horse of yours is mixed up in it. I wish Jerry'd never taken you with him to the stockyards that day."

After that, Peter tried to do his schooling when there were not many customers around; but by early summer Dick Stearns said it was time for someone else to try the black.

"Let's raise the jumps to four feet and try him with a rider. I'll take him over this time, but I can't promise to be your practice boy very often. We'd better pick out one of the best students and get him to do it. Can't think who on earth it would be though."

Peter expected Charcoal to work extra well under Dick, but the colt seemed indifferent. "Looks like he's going to be a one-man horse," the young instructor said surprisedly. Twice more that week he tried it, but Charcoal gave only mediocre performances.

"He doesn't dislike me," Dick finally said, puzzled. "But he doesn't cotton to me either. I don't believe he'll ever really exert himself for me. He's an odd horse, Peter . . . but smarter than most. Try to find someone else he takes to a lot. Then he'll jump his heart out. But I'm the only one around right now to get him started. We'll raise the bars to four and a half feet just this once to see what happens."

Peter swelled with pride as he saw the black sail over the higher jump with plenty to spare. Watching the rippling muscles under the glossy black hide, the graceful, slender neck and head, the brilliant white streak between wide, intelligent eyes, and the trim, straight legs, he realized that Charcoal had come a long ways in ten months. The colt surely must have good blood lines. The mystery of his parentage tantalized Peter. He wished there were some way to solve it. Charcoal's disposition had improved too. Ever since he had been gelded early in the spring, he had gradually become less excitable, less inclined to nip, and generally more tractable. Now they could turn one of the mares or other geldings into the big yard with him for company, and he no longer roamed the fence restlessly or tried to jump it.

The garden damage had been settled by the tactful Jerry for less than twenty-five dollars all told—an amount Peter wanted to repay as soon as possible. It seemed as if his other debts were mounting up until he never in the world would be able to pay his father back for Charcoal. Every time he got a few dollars ahead, there were items like the gelding, the shoeing, more feed to buy, or some essential item of clothing or school expense for himself. But Peter made up his mind he wouldn't rest until the black was his own.

The problem of finding a rider for Charcoal hung fire. In the meantime Peter continued to give him his daily exercise, both under the saddle and over the liberty jumps. But Charcoal needed to be schooled over the jumps with a rider. Peter begged his Dad to let him try it, but both parents firmly said no. Dick was too busy to spend more than an hour or two a week with the colt, and there was not a single advanced rider to whom they could trust Charcoal as yet.

"The few riders that could handle your horse," Dick told Peter regretfully, "have jumpers of their own to exercise constantly and keep in show trim. I've asked, and none of them will take on an extra."

The situation seemed to have struck an impasse. Peter knew there was one person, and one alone, who could handle Charcoal at this stage of his training— Dodo Haynes. Mr. Haynes owned and showed several types of horses: five-gaited, three-gaited, fine harness, Tennessee Walkers, and jumpers. He prided himself on having an entry in practically every class in the various northwest shows. Dodo could ride anything. If only she could ride the black for Peter now!

But Dodo was a long ways off. True, he had written her about the black; but he had never thought to ask her for a visit. If she came it could only be for a short time, and the solution would be only temporary. Yet, it was worth a try. With renewed hope Peter rushed into the kitchen and proposed the idea to his mother.

"Of course we'd be glad to have Dodo," Mrs. Morgan said. "If she comes though, you've got to do something besides train the colt, so she'll be sure to have a good time. You'll have to take time out for movies or a picnic now and then."

Before Dodo had time to answer Peter's invitation, John Morgan called him into the office one afternoon.

"Peter, the word's going around that you really need help in schooling Charcoal. I've had six or eight of the students in here pestering me for a chance at him. I referred them to you; but they all said it was no use asking, because you and Dick would turn them down. They don't like it. They think that any horse that's yours or mine is Academy property and open to all riders. Remember what happened in regard to Connie Pearson? We lost at least five good, steady riders by your refusal to let her ride your horse. I've decided to put some of the better students up on Charcoal."

Mounting resentment brought a hot flush to Peter's cheeks. It was a bitter pill to have his father lay down the law about Charcoal, even though he himself had been worried about the problem of a rider. To have someone not of his own choosing step in and reap the benefit after he had spent countless hours and days training the colt was hard to take too. Dick had agreed that none of the advanced riders was good enough to take on the job, and Dick knew more about jumpers than his Dad. Only a few of the private owners with show jumpers of their own could have handled Charcoal, and they had refused.

"Did you talk to Dick?" Peter asked angrily. "It'll ruin Charcoal . . . spoil everything."

"Yes, I did." John Morgan paused. "He wasn't very enthusiastic, I'll admit; but he doesn't have the final responsibility for building up this business, nor do you. Sometimes we have to sacrifice our individual desires, Peter, for the common good. From now on you'll have to leave it to my judgment who schools

Charcoal . . . and how often. You can continue to ride him in between for exercise, just as you do now."

Peter flushed. His jaw set stubbornly. "But, Dad, he's *my* horse. You're taking him away from me, maybe ruining him. He's a one-man horse. Dick says so himself."

John Morgan seldom broke his usual calm, but now, again, sudden and unexpected anger flared up in his eyes.

"You're talking to me as if I were the son and you the father, as if I had no judgment concerning horses. Charcoal is technically mine. I paid for him, and this once I'm going to take advantage of the situation. In everything up to now you've had your way; but I was working with horses for years before you were born, and I think you ought to trust me. That's all. I'll move Charcoal into the main stable, keep him up in a stall, and have him thoroughly groomed every day. He's used to stalls now; and I doubt he'll cause any trouble, particularly with horses on all sides for company."

Peter got up and walked out. His hands were clenched at his sides, and he bit his tongue to keep back a sharp retort. His father was unfair. What had come over him? Bewildered and angry, Peter sought out Dick.

"Well." Dick scratched his head. "There's not much we can do. After all he's boss, and he's your father.

We *could* be wrong. Maybe some of those riders will get along with Charcoal all right."

"But," Peter muttered disgustedly, "I've just written to Dodo. Why couldn't Dad wait and give her a chance first?"

"Your Dad's not thinking just of the colt. He's thinking about the future of the Academy, and ultimately the future of you and your mother. Your Dad's a fine man, Peter. Whatever he does, it's because he thinks it's best for everybody."

But Peter was not to be comforted. He went out and stared at Charcoal for a long time in the gathering dusk. He ate his supper in silence and went to bed early, still feeling hard and resentful.

CHAPTER VII

Enter Dodo

For the next few days Peter was completely miserable. When Dodo's letter finally came, he scanned it quickly with a feeling it didn't really matter now. Yet it somehow gave him a lift.

Dear Peter:
Thanks for asking me. Dad and Mother are going for a cruise along the California coast in June, and I'm supposed to go along. Also have to ride in two horse shows, one before the cruise, one after. But I'll come in July if you still want me. I have an aunt in your town, you know. I'll have to spend part of the time with her, but I'll come over and ride with you every day anyway.

Peter wondered if he ought to write her about everyone else being given a chance at Charcoal first. Maybe then she wouldn't want to come. But he needed her worse than ever, if only to sympathize.

Through Dick or one of the stablemen, Peter found out whenever anyone was slated to ride Charcoal. He didn't want to ask his father. In fact, he and the elder Morgan were hardly on speaking terms. Yet Peter was determined not to make the first move at reconciliation, and inwardly he was worrying about an entirely new problem. Even if he could raise the thirty dollars for Charcoal now, he doubted that his father, in his present mood, would sell him for any such sum. Bitterness welled up in him all over again at the thought.

He wished they were back in Glen Valley, with John Morgan a private trainer again and the three of them living on the little farm next to the Haynes place. Then they'd be out of this worry and strain of business that seemed to change his father so. Peter wanted to talk the whole problem over with his mother; but she'd probably agree with his father, outwardly at least.

Whenever someone new rode Charcoal, Peter was always up in the ringside seats watching. He just couldn't stay away even though it was torture to be there. He held his breath each time a rider mounted, but Charcoal usually behaved better than he expected. The gelding didn't put himself out for any of them; but he didn't try to throw them either, and his occasional show of high spirits was no more than was to be expected from any young horse well fed and full of life.

One afternoon as he sat watching, Peter heard footsteps coming up behind him—and his father's voice cut in on his thoughts.

"You see, Peter, it isn't going so badly, is it? If I admit you were right about Charcoal having real promise, will you admit I was right to let him get this extra schooling under a variety of riders?"

Peter was silent for a moment. This was only the beginning. The real test of the black's training would come next year, and the next.

"I don't know," he told his father dully. "I don't know."

Sensing his unhappiness, John Morgan did not press the point. Peter turned and watched as his father walked away. They seemed miles apart in understanding.

Peter's only chance at Charcoal these days was a short ride every other day or so. Now they went out on the trails so that the black would get used to strange sights and sounds. He shied occasionally as something unexpected blew across the path or a chipmunk or a rabbit ran out of the underbrush, but he was very sensible on the whole. Peter found himself talking to him as he so often did to Star, almost as if the horse were human.

At the end of the first week in July, Dodo arrived,

pert and freckle-faced, full of fun as always, but a little older, a little more sedate. Peter noticed the difference at once. He wondered if Dodo saw any difference in him. Of course her first words were of the black gelding.

"Lead me to him."

The elder Morgans were busy welcoming Mr. and Mrs. Haynes, so Peter took her right to the indoor ring. He led the colt out and put him over the liberty jumps on the longe line while Dodo watched fascinated. Her eyes widened with appreciation. "Peter, he's wonderful!" She came down into the ring and Charcoal nosed at her hand and begged for a tidbit. Peter was surprised. The colt just tolerated most people. It was seldom he responded or made advances on his own.

"He likes you," Peter said, a curious thread of hope and excitement in his voice.

"Peter, you're the luckiest mortal alive. To think of finding a treasure like this in a bunch of wild horses! You've done wonders with him. How about me trying him first thing tomorrow?"

"O.K., if he isn't already promised to someone." Shamefacedly Peter told her of the trouble with his father and the way Charcoal was being used. "I wish we'd never bought this darn Riding Academy," he concluded disgustedly. "So far those riders haven't hurt Charcoal, but just give them time. Only the best have had a whack at him up to now."

"I wish you were back in Glen Valley," Dodo mused. "Our new trainer's all right in some ways, but he's not very reliable and not nearly as nice as your Dad. And of course I can see how your Dad might like being in business for himself."

Fortunately no one had asked for Charcoal in the morning, so Dodo and Peter had him all to themselves. Dodo was staying with the Morgans the first week and with her aunt the second, so she appeared at breakfast all dressed in her riding clothes. Peter saddled and bridled the black, himself, with special care. Dodo stood at Charcoal's head talking to him and rubbing his neck. Twice he nuzzled her, and his dark, liquid eyes were soft with approval. Peter gave her a leg up and then settled down on the bleachers to watch.

Charcoal wanted to head for the jumps right away, but Dodo checked him.

"I want to get the feel of him first," she called up to Peter. "I'm going outside."

She rode out through the gate and around the grounds. It wasn't long before she was back, her eyes shining. Charcoal was moving with a natural joy and freedom such as Peter had never seen. He had felt a degree of it when he was in the saddle himself, but seeing it from the ground was a new experience. The black gelding looked every inch an aristocrat.

"Here we go!" Dodo yelled.

She turned Charcoal into the course. He soared over the jumps in perfect form, with hind legs tucked up neatly, landing easily and with unbroken stride. Dodo sat him beautifully.

"Hold everything!" Peter barked as she started another round. "I want Dick Stearns to see this."

Dick came at his excited request and watched girl and horse twice around the course. "This is it!" he told Peter decisively. "They're perfect together. Can't you keep that girl here somehow?"

"I'm afraid not, but maybe we could send Charcoal to her. I'm going after Dad."

John Morgan dropped what he was doing and followed Pete in silence to the ring. Dodo took the gelding around twice more. John Morgan sat quietly until Dodo began walking the colt to calm him down. Charcoal was up on his toes, straining at the bit, anxious to jump again.

"I see what you mean," Peter's father said slowly. "They're wonderful together, no doubt about it . . . but Dodo can't stay on after school starts. So where does that leave you? We'll just have to go on looking for the best rider here to develop your horse. Sorry, son. Wish you could understand that trying to make a riding academy pay and please everybody isn't easy."

Peter and Dodo were jubilant. Her enthusiasm over Charcoal brought Peter renewed faith and pride.

"If I could talk Dad into letting me pay for him, would your Dad board him this winter—and you work him for me? I can earn enough from my paper route to pay his keep; that is, I think I can."

"Oh, Dad will take him if I want him to." Dodo's voice was just as excited as Peter's. "That's a swell idea! And don't worry—Dad won't charge very much if you'll promise to let me ride Charcoal at his first show. Maybe next season when he's five we could enter him. How about it?"

Peter looked at her gratefully. "You're a peach, Dodo. But the big rub is that I don't own him yet. It all depends on who wins out for control of him—Dad or me. It oughtn't to be that way, Dodo. He and I ought to be able to get together on it."

"Would it do any good if I talked to him, or maybe if Dad talked to him?"

"No." Peter's eyes were somber. "It's strictly a family affair. Thanks just the same."

Dodo spent the afternoon at her aunt's, and in the evening she and Peter went to a movie. Mrs. Morgan told Dodo to sleep late, mornings.

"I'll let you get your own breakfast. That way you'll feel free to stay in bed as long as you like."

So when Dodo awakened on the second morning after her arrival, looked at her watch, and saw that it was eight o'clock, she rolled over for another hour or two of sleep. Peter strolled by her closed bedroom door. There was not a sound, so he decided he might as well go on out to the stable. In the corridor between the stalls he met Bob carrying Charcoal's saddle and bridle over his arm.

"Whew!" Peter said surprisedly. "Who's riding Charcoal so early?"

Bob slowed his pace and went into the stall as if he hadn't heard. Peter followed and leaned against the stall door, talking gently to the black.

"You might as well tell me," he persisted. "I'll be out there watching anyway. Why on earth did somebody have to ask for him this morning? I wanted to keep him fresh for Dodo."

Bob turned slowly, avoiding Peter's gaze. "Don't go out there, Pete. Your Dad doesn't want you to. He's gone to the house to tell you. It's Connie Pearson."

"Connie Pearson!"

Peter felt as if someone had slapped him full in the face. "But I thought she was through with us. The rest were bad enough . . . but Connie Pearson! I'm going to watch. If Dad wants me out of there, he'll have to throw me out. But he doesn't need to worry. I won't say a word to his precious little customer. Where's she working—inside or out?"

"Inside," Bob said. He sounded scared. "I guess Connie heard that everybody was riding Charcoal now, and she decided to come back and have a try at it. Gives her a chance to have her way after all, even if she can't be the first."

Heartsick and angry, Peter hurried toward the ring. He limped a little more than usual, a sure sign he was disturbed. Climbing up to the top row of seats, he slumped down and stared morosely at the big doors through which horse and rider must soon appear.

CHAPTER VIII

Disaster

Peter stared unhappily at the door. He was perspiring and jittery, although the interior of the building was still cool from the night air. Bob finally appeared, leading Charcoal—and there was Connie Pearson, already in the saddle.

Bob loosed his hold at the door. "Good luck," he said, and disappeared.

Connie did not immediately look up and see Peter. Her mind was on her mount. She seemed to be having trouble deciding just how tight to hold the reins, and Charcoal, sensing her uncertainty, moved uneasily. Peter wanted to call out to her, but he didn't dare. She'd probably be mad enough when she noticed he was there. It was mighty careless of his father, he thought, to let her work the colt the first time alone. Just as he felt his anger mounting again, Dick Stearns appeared at his elbow. The assistant riding master laid a quick hand on Peter's shoulder.

"I know it's tough, Pete. But we're both here now

to keep an eye out. You just grin and bear it. I'll coach her."

Dick's attention had been momentarily on Peter. For just a few seconds neither of them had been watching Connie. In that brief moment she saw them and, anxious to prove she could handle him without help, set the black at the jumps. Peter and Dick turned at the sound of thudding hoofs. Charcoal was only a few feet from the take-off. Suddenly Peter froze with horror. The bars were at least a foot higher than usual. Someone practicing with one of the show jumpers, unusually late the night before, had raised the bars and failed to lower them again.

"Stop!" he yelled frenziedly, but it was too late.

Charcoal was already in the air. Connie's position was bad, her weight all wrong. In that split second Peter strained every nerve and sinew along with the black. Charcoal's hind hoofs caught the top bars and sent it rolling. He could have cleared the five feet easily if he'd been conditioned to it slowly, but all spring and summer he'd jumped four feet or less. Mind and muscles were schooled for that particular height.

As the black hit the ground with a thud, so unlike his usual springy landing, Peter jumped up, yelling at Connie to stop. She heard him and began tugging on the reins. Dick ran down the row of seats toward the ring. But there was no stopping Charcoal now. He had been taught to make the rounds, and he was halfway to the next jump. Peter sank back and gripped the edge of the seat with his hands. He knew Dick couldn't stop the colt . . . no one could. Charcoal had done six feet the year before when he cleared the paddock fence, but that was with a much longer take-off and no rider.

Charcoal was safely over the second jump before Peter could organize his thoughts. The black had learned that more was required of him; this time the top rail stayed in place. Though he was angry and worried, Peter was thrilled at the way the colt cleared that second jump, even though his rider was more of a hindrance than a help.

At the third take-off Charcoal seemed to lack his usual buoyancy. He struck the top rail with one front hoof and literally fell over the jump. Then it all happened so fast Peter sat there dazed, unable to move. The colt crashed as he came down, tossing Connie into the soft tanbark ten or twelve feet ahead. He struggled to rise and finally came up; but he stood on three legs, holding the right front hoof in the air.

Dick ran to Connie and helped her to her feet. She was bruised and shaken, but otherwise unhurt. His temporary paralysis over, Peter rushed down into the arena. Charcoal stood with dangling reins, making no effort to move. Peter picked up the reins and soothed the trembling colt. Charcoal was shaking all over from nervousness and fright.

"Get the vet, quick," Peter called to Dick. "I'll stay with him."

Connie glared at him before she turned to walk stiffly out of the arena. Peter heard her mutter something about "more worried about the darned horse than he is about me."

"Don't worry, boy," Peter begged anxiously, stroking Charcoal's forehead. Quick tears of rage and discouragement sprang to his eyes. It was all so useless. This wouldn't have happened if it hadn't been for Connie Pearson. Anyone else would have taken it more carefully, noted at once that the jumps were wrong.

It seemed an eternity before his father and Dodo appeared. John Morgan's eyes were serious, and he did not look directly at Peter.

"No use to tell you how sorry I am," he said. "Dr. Gray will be here right away. I hope it's nothing serious."

"It better not be," Peter muttered. "A jumper's no good without good legs, and Charcoal's whole life is his jumping."

Sensing Peter's misery and the strain between father and son, Dodo didn't talk but stood by Charcoal stroking his neck. John Morgan stooped to look at the injured foot. Peter flashed a look of gratitude at Dodo for her unspoken sympathy.

Finally the genial veterinary hurried in through the

big doors, his little black bag under his arm. He examined Charcoal's entire leg from the shoulder down. Finally he hit a spot so tender the horse crouched and jerked his hoof away. With infinite patience Dr. Gray retrieved it and worked around the spot very gently.

When he had finished he stood up, his expression grave. He turned to Peter. "I'm afraid it's a pulled tendon. That means he may never jump again. On the other hand, with just the right combination of rest and care, he might recover completely. These conditions are sometimes unpredictable. Right now he must be kept absolutely quiet in a stall, with frequent hot Epsom-salts compresses. Later, when he is able to get around better, he should be turned into a nice green pasture with a good deep mudhole somewhere in it. If he were tied so he'd have to stand in it a couple of hours a day, it might help. We'll do what we can; then we'll have to let Nature take her course. Try to get him to his stall now. He can make it on three legs if you can coax him into trying."

Peter felt himself grow cold at the doctor's words. Charcoal was one of those rare cases in a hundred—a born jumper. Condemning him to the prosaic life of a saddle horse would be like grounding a born airplane pilot.

Peter took the reins and tugged gently. Charcoal looked at him with worried eyes, not knowing how to respond. Suddenly Dr. Gray slapped him lightly on the haunches. Startled, Charcoal lunged forward on three legs. Peter encouraged him. The doctor flourished a strap he carried in his case. Charcoal saw the motion out of the corner of his eye and made another halting step. Again Peter praised him. Slowly, by dint of much urging and pulling, they got the colt back to his stall. John Morgan had gone silently about his business, and Peter was glad. Dick had come to help and they two worked with the doctor perfectly.

"Well!" Dodo said ruefully after Dr. Gray had soaked the injured foot and bound it up. "Guess I'm not going to be able to do you much good after all, Peter. There'll be no training of Charcoal for a while."

"Or ever maybe," Peter said angrily. "Stick around awhile, please, Dodo. We can ride every day. I'll lend you Star if you like and I'll ride one of the Academy horses. I've got an idea, and I want to see if we can't work it out before you go."

A sudden gleam came into Dodo's eye. "I'll bet I know what you mean. The doctor said later . . . a good green pasture, didn't he, and a good mudhole? Remember the lower pasture on our place, where that little stream runs through? It's beautiful and shady, and there's always mud along the bank where the horses come down to drink. No need to even create a mudhole. It's just the thing. But will your Dad let him go?"

"I think he will . . . now," Peter said grimly. "After all he's no use to his precious riders this way."

Dodo put a comforting hand on his arm. "Don't be so bitter, Peter. Your Dad has to make a living. But, just between you and me, I don't like the way he looks. He's so much thinner, has so many more worry lines on his face than when he worked for Dad. Is the business going badly?"

"I don't know. At first it did. Then it was lots better. I don't know. Maybe just lately . . ."

Suddenly he realized that he had left his father out on a limb, adding to his worries instead of trying to help. But, he told himself angrily, sacrificing Charcoal to the cause had seemed so utterly needless.

That evening Dodo was away at her aunt's for dinner. Toward the end of their own meal, Peter turned to his father. He knew there were no evening classes to call him away immediately on this particular night.

"Can I talk to you a minute?"

"Sure. Anything your mother shouldn't hear?"

"No." Peter flushed. He hadn't meant to exclude his mother, just spare her if the discussion ended in a quarrel. "Well, now that Charcoal's hurt and just a liability around here, can I pay you the thirty and own him myself? I can give you fifteen now and five the first of each month when I collect from my route."

John Morgan winced at his tone. "I don't quite like

the way you put it," he said, "but you can *have* the horse, Peter. I meant to give him to you sooner or later anyway."

"I don't want him as a gift," Peter said stiffly. "I'd rather pay the thirty dollars, or whatever you think he's worth."

John Morgan hesitated. He wanted terribly to get through to Peter, but he couldn't. He looked helplessly at his wife and then back at his son. His shoulders sagged. "Sometimes," he said wearily, "I wonder if it's any use, all of this . . ." He motioned toward the big shape of the Academy outside their window . . . the general surroundings. "Go ahead," he told Peter. "Take the horse for thirty dollars. Then maybe we'll have an end to all this misunderstanding."

Gravely Peter took out his billfold and counted out three five-dollar bills. He handed his father a scrap of paper on which he had written:

I promise to pay to John Morgan fifteen dollars ($15) balance on one black gelding named Charcoal, breeding unknown.
SIGNED—Peter Morgan

Just as gravely his father took the bills and the note. Elizabeth Morgan watched them anxiously.

Peter's eyes lighted. "Now can I do exactly as I please with Charcoal?"

"Exactly as you please," his father said heavily. He rose and walked out of the room.

Peter was conscious that his mother had come over beside him. She reached out suddenly and pressed his head against her breast.

"Oh, Peter." She caught her breath with a sob. "You two are all I have. Why must you be hurting each other so?"

CHAPTER IX

Home Town Visit

Dodo stayed on for three weeks, and having her around cheered Peter considerably. The veterinary treated Charcoal often until he was able to put the injured foot to the ground and move about. He had a limp and the doctor pointed out that it would be a good long while before he got over it. Even then there would be a weakness in the tendon which very likely would interfere with jumping.

Dodo wrote to her father, and a letter came back promptly saying by all means to bring the black gelding home with her. Mr. Haynes even offered to transport him, saying he had to come after Dodo anyway and would bring along a horse trailer. He also suggested that Peter go back with them for the next two weeks.

Of course the paper route had to be taken care of before Peter could visit the Hayneses. He and Dodo went together to Hank Elkins, but only after they had begged him, almost on bended knees, did he consent to substitute.

"Here there's only two weeks of summer vacation left," he grumbled, "and you two expect me to drag out of bed practically at daybreak every morning so you can go off and have a good time."

"Come on. Be a good sport," Peter urged. "After all, who took the route off your hands in the first place?"

Dodo flashed Hank a winning smile. "Maybe if Peter comes to visit us next summer you could come along," she urged.

That did it. Hank got the list of new subscribers and promised to be on the job for sure.

The trip to Glen Valley was fairly uneventful; but as they came closer, Peter became very thoughtful. He wondered how it would seem to stay at the Hayneses', in the big house he had always admired. Seeing someone else living in the familiar cozy cottage where he had been born, knowing he could never go back to it, would be hard.

As the library building came into view, Peter exclaimed, "Gee, Mr. Haynes, there's the library! And it's open! Would you mind stopping just a minute while I say hello to Miss Robbins?"

Mr. Haynes drew up in front of the neat little building that housed a branch of the county library. Peter hurried in through the wide, friendly door, glad that the brown-haired, stocky lady at the charging desk was too busy to look up. Her back was toward him and he tiptoed up behind her, smiling broadly.

"Hi, Miss Robbins! How about a new horse book?"

The little librarian jumped up, startled; then, before the embarrassed Peter could protest, she threw her arms around him and gave him a big hug.

"Peter Morgan, you rascal! If *that* didn't sound natural! As a matter of fact, we've got quite a few new horse books since you moved away; but I'll bet you've gotten them all at that big city library of yours. After all, they've got just thousands of books."

"Maybe so. Maybe so." Peter leaned back against the desk and surveyed the cheerful little room fondly. "But I've not found anyone as nice as you, Miss Robbins, and the nearest branch library is a long ways from the Riding Academy. I don't have time to get there very often any more. You used to get me any book I wanted from the state library. What more could anyone ask?"

The genial little woman beamed at his praise. "And what are you doing here, Peter? Don't tell me you're back to stay?"

"I wish I were. But it's just a visit with the Hayneses. Is Miss Pepper still here?"

"Yes. I heard she just got back to town last Saturday. Came a little early. Likely you'll see her. And Dr. Bush will have a fit if you don't go to see him. He's a mighty good friend to you."

"I know it!" Peter's voice was warm. "Why, if it

hadn't been for Doc Bush getting all those people to-gether and having the sale, I'd never have had Star. Well, I'd better be getting on, Miss Robbins. If I run out of something to do up at the Hayneses', I'll come down and borrow a book."

"See that you do. I'll have one all picked out. You look so much taller and handsomer, I hardly knew you. And how about your drawing, Peter? You were so good at it. I hope you haven't neglected it."

Peter blushed. "Well, to tell you the truth, I haven't had much time, but I still like it. As for being taller, after all I'm fourteen now. I'll be in to see you again. I've brought a horse to the Haynes farm. Hope you'll come over and see him."

At the Haynes farm Charcoal was very carefully unloaded. The stableman had prepared a big box stall, deep with clean, sweet-smelling straw. Stiff from his long ride, the black gelding limped even more than usual. Peter too, stiff from sitting so long, walked with a noticeable limp. The stableman was new.

Seeing his curious glance and reading his unspoken thoughts, Peter spoke wryly.

"Yep, we're both lame. Two of a kind." Then, not-ing the stableman's embarrassment, he regretted his words.

＊　　＊　　＊　　＊　　＊

Peter's two weeks at the Hayneses' passed all too quickly. There were visits to the kindly Dr. Bush, who had done so much for him; Miss Pepper, the sixth-grade teacher, who had encouraged him with his art; all his old school friends, and even the storekeepers in the little town. Dodo and he rode her beautiful Palomino parade horse and a good Tennessee Walking mare Mr. Haynes had bought in order to raise a few colts.

Every day Peter bathed Charcoal's foot and kept hot compresses on it for half an hour. Then he led the colt back and forth in the small stableyard, forcing him to take a little exercise. Since it was still painful to put any weight on the injured tendon, Charcoal was inclined to stand still whenever he could; and that, of course, caused the foot to stiffen.

"By the time I go, you'll be able to turn him out in the big pasture," Peter told Dodo. "Dr. Gray said it wouldn't be necessary to treat him any more, after that, unless he gets much worse. I'll show you just what to do in case that happens, and I'll leave all the rest of the medicine the vet gave me."

Peter watched hopefully for signs of improvement. If there were any, he failed to see them; and by the end of the two weeks he was decidedly discouraged.

"But the vet said it would be a slow process," Dodo reminded him. "Now you quit worrying. I'll take good care of Charcoal, and I'll write you every week about him. When the cold weather comes, we'll bring him in to the barn nights and turn him out in the small stableyard on good days. I'll think you don't trust me if you don't stop fussing. As for the board, Dad says ten dollars a month is plenty. We raise a lot of our own feed, and the rest we buy in large quantities. He'll be on pasture part of the time too. Come spring, Charcoal will probably be absolutely O.K. and I'll be schooling him."

The last day was the hardest. Peter hated saying goodbye to everyone, especially the Hayneses and Charcoal. The black and he had become closer since he had taken so much time to care for the injured tendon. But deep down he knew that no horse, even Charcoal, would mean as much to him as Star.

That last day Peter sat propped against a tree, staring at the black gelding, pencil, drawing board, and paper in his lap. Dodo came quietly up behind him and peeked over his shoulder.

"How are you coming? I've been wondering why you've never done a sketch of Charcoal. Or have you?"

"Nope. Too busy training him. Couldn't seem to get just the idea I was after, either. Now I've decided I want to do him just as he is today, lame foot and all. Standing there under that tree, weight on three legs, head at half-mast, and perfectly relaxed . . . that's the way I want him now. Someday I want to make another drawing of him by contrast, a picture from life . . . Charcoal in action . . . head up, ears forward, body tensed, going over a jump as if he's headed for the moon."

Suddenly Peter gripped Dodo's arm. His fingers dug into it until she winced with pain. "Dodo, that's the way it's got to be . . . someday. You and I have got to bring him back."

"We will." Dodo spoke firmly, her eyes shining at the mental image he had conjured up. "Don't worry, Peter, we will. Now go ahead and finish your sketch so you can take it home and have it to remind you of Charcoal. Make it a good one!"

CHAPTER X

A Visit to the Doctor

The drawing of Charcoal *was* good; everyone who saw it thought so. During the lonely months of fall and winter following his return home, that picture was a sort of talisman to Peter. He tacked it up in his room, and every time he looked at it he knew that somehow, *some way*, the black gelding *must* get well.

True to her word, Dodo wrote often. She reported constant, if slow, improvement. When the really cold weather set in, business at the Riding Academy fell off to the point where John Morgan had to discharge Dick Stearns. It was a blow to Peter, because the young assistant had been a real ally. Soon afterward Peter's father spoke to him one morning at breakfast.

"I want you to help teach. You can handle regular beginning students individually and assist me with the classes, either on Star or working from the ground. How about it?"

"I don't know." Peter looked at his father in surprise. "I'm afraid your riders wouldn't trust anybody so young."

John Morgan looked displeased. "I think I'm a better judge of that than you. I'll pay you, but not as much as an experienced teacher."

Peter flushed. It wasn't the money that made him hesitate, and his Dad should have known it. "It's not that. I just don't think I know enough. Then I wanted to bring Charcoal home in the spring, work with him, and enter him in some of the local shows if I can get Dodo to ride him."

"Always Charcoal!" John Morgan's voice was impatient. "Peter, why don't you face the facts? That horse will probably never be able to jump again. Settle down and help me make a go of this stable. You've been sort of in a dream world ever since you came across that black broomtail."

Peter turned away. There was that term of scorn again—"broomtail." His father just wouldn't understand. Back in the old days they could have sat down and talked it out. Now it seemed as if John Morgan thought of nothing in the world but the business and money-making.

Peter tried to help with the teaching, but he was never very sure of himself. He knew how to ride, but it was hard for him to tell others. He took to talking aloud to Star on the morning newspaper route, telling the big horse his troubles, drawing a measure of comfort from the way Star cocked his ears back and nodded his head wisely in rhythm with his easy, gliding walk. All good walking horses nod their heads like that in time to their motion, but to Peter it seemed as if Star understood and sympathized. Certainly the stallion had never behaved better or been more responsive.

The winter dragged slowly along. During his second year in junior high Peter enrolled in an art class, finding some outlet for his impatience and discontent in drawing. He opened each letter from Dodo with trembling hands, fearful it would carry the news of a setback for Charcoal. Sometimes she said so little that Peter could have shaken her. Then, just when he would begin to fear things were not going well, a reassuring letter would come. After that Peter would walk on the clouds for a few days, and gradually the tension eased out of him as successive reports indicated a gradual but steady progress.

As winter moved inevitably toward spring and there was much talk around the stable of the coming horse shows, Peter began to get the show fever too. Several times he caught himself dreaming about Charcoal sailing over the jumps, making an amazing record, silencing forever the doubters who called him "broomtail."

Early spring brought some improvement in business and John Morgan seemed more like his old self. The winter had been an unusually hard one. Almost steady rain had kept the outdoor riders off the trails, and cold weather in between had cut classes to a minimum in the big unheated indoor ring. Only the considerable number of boarders and a few extra private pupils who turned up kept things going, but Peter knew that the payments were way behind. John Morgan had gone about tense and silent, until there was an added sense of strain in the house and stable.

Then came the day when he smiled at Peter and said, "Well, son, maybe we can swing it after all, with you helping."

The unusual sudden warmth in his tone comforted Peter and helped to heal the breach between them. "Guess I'd better be getting off to school," he said awkwardly, turning to gather up his books. He stopped short as his father spoke again.

There was amazement and congratulation in John Morgan's voice. "Peter, do you know you're not limping at all? I can't remember that you've limped for weeks. Good for you! Write Doc Bush and tell him about it."

Peter realized with almost a sense of shock that his father was right. He had been so busy with school, the paper route, his work at the stable, and thinking and writing about Charcoal, there had been no time at all to think about himself. The improvement had been so gradual he couldn't remember exactly when his hip had last bothered him. Turning suddenly didn't hurt any more, or going down steps, or mounting a horse. And lately, come to think of it, he had been bearing his weight in both stirrups and not depending on the specially built leather handle on the front of his saddle.

Peter nodded happily. "I'll write the Doc tonight."

During the bus ride into town his mind leaped dizzily ahead, daring to dream of the possibilities a real cure might open to him. If Charcoal got well and his own cure proved permanent, what was to prevent *him* from riding the black over the jumps? What would stand between *him* and the shows? Peter couldn't wait to write Dr. Bush. He stole time out of his first study hour to scribble the message on a sheet from his notebook, talked the secretary in the school office into selling him a stamped envelope, and then mailed it at the corner letter box. That done, he tried somewhat unsuccessfully to settle down to work. He had grown so accustomed to that bad hip that he had taken it for granted it might never get well. Now a new world seemed to open out before him.

Three days later an answering letter came from the doctor. "I'd like to look you over," it said. "I've always hoped your old injury would heal completely; but I don't want you to get your hopes too high till I can make an examination, and until several months have passed with no recurrence of pain or trouble. Could you possibly come down during your spring vacation, which must be very near? This time there's to be no fee for my services."

Peter showed the letter to his folks. A visit to Dr. Bush meant a visit to the Hayneses and getting to check on Charcoal's condition, but he thought it best not to mention that. He could hardly wait while his father slowly read the letter aloud, his mother listening intently.

"What do you think?" John Morgan asked his wife. "I just can't get away to drive Pete to Glen Valley. Bob and I haven't time to stop and cook our own meals now, either, if you take him. Things are just opening up, here, but we've got to give the Doc a chance to check up on this. Pete, you'll just have to go by yourself on the bus. The fare will be a bit of a problem, but we'll manage."

Peter was so tickled he could hardly talk. "Don't worry about the fare. I've got enough left over from paying Charcoal's board and my other expenses this month to buy my own ticket. And you notice Dr. Bush says he won't charge anything."

"Bless his heart," Mrs. Morgan said gratefully. "They just don't come any finer." She turned to Peter. "Can you stay at the Hayneses'?"

"Sure. Dodo said I was welcome any time, and you remember her Dad said so too. I'll write her I'm coming."

"You'll only need to stay a day or two," his father reminded him. "I'll need you here badly. With school closed for spring vacation we might have a rush of business, and Heaven knows we need it."

Momentarily sobered, Peter promised—although he couldn't suppress a feeling of resentment against the Riding Academy. There it was, getting in his way again, keeping him from staying as long as he'd like to. For the next two weeks he was in seventh heaven. He didn't write Dodo after all. He knew it would be all right to go, and he wanted to surprise her.

The day Peter arrived in Glen Valley, spring was out in full force. The sun warmed his bare head as he walked down the familiar street swinging his cap. Daffodils and hyacinths were pushing up through the moist, dark earth, bursting into bloom. There were even a few birds in the trees above him, chirping and fussing as if to welcome him. Peter passed by the little library, not daring to look in. He'd see Miss Robbins later, and Dr. Bush too. Right now there was only one thing on his mind—Charcoal.

In his haste Peter forgot to cross the street, go around the block, or otherwise avoid Dr. Bush's office. He was suddenly startled by a loud tapping and looked up to see the doctor smiling down through the big front window of his office, motioning him inside. There was nothing to do but turn and go in.

"Thought you'd be getting in on this bus, so I was watching for you," the doctor said heartily. "Wanted to come meet you, but I was held up with a patient. She just left a few seconds ago. I figured you'd come straight here anyway. Want to stay at my place tonight?"

"Oh no, thanks. I promised to go to the Hayneses'."

The doctor glanced at his appointment book. "Might as well examine you now. No one coming for half an hour, and they can wait a while if necessary. Come on in and get ready."

To Peter it was an old story. The doctor had examined him every few months now for several years. But when he got into the inside examination room, he stopped short in surprise. There was a huge machine that took up half the office.

The doctor stood beaming at it. "Something new, boy. My own X-ray. Always had to send my patients up to the county seat or the hospital. Now I can do it right here. Had to take a special short course in how to work the thing, but I've got it down pat now. Come on and undress. I'm going to really give you the once-over."

Peter had never had such a thorough examination in his life. After the X-rays the doctor pushed and pulled and prodded, felt his hip and thigh up and down and right and left, made him walk and turn, step up and down, lie on his back and roll and twist. Peter did it all without a twinge. The doctor developed the X-rays, while Peter sat in the waiting room on pins and needles. He hardly knew which was more important to him, to know the results of the examination or to see Charcoal.

Finally the doctor appeared and Peter almost

jumped from his chair in spite of the fact that there were two strangers in the waiting room by now.

"Tell me quick, Doc."

The doctor put an arm around his shoulder. "As far as I can see you're fit as a fiddle. The pictures show that your hip is as normal as anybody's. I've got the pictures taken at the hospital when you were first hurt, and I tell you, boy, you wouldn't know it was the same hip. You've made a very rapid recovery, even though it may have seemed slow and painful to you. Only one out of ten cases of the kind ever come out as well as you have. In order not to tempt Providence though, I want you to be careful for at least two months more and to report immediately if the pain or tenderness comes back. If not, after that you can resume most of your normal activities. Don't go out for football though. It's a little too rugged. You might throw something out of place again."

Peter strode out of the office, down the street, and out on the country road as if he were walking on air. Past the old place he went, with only a quick look, whistling loudly. The long trek up the hill to the Haynes place that had once seemed so hard was nothing now.

CHAPTER XI

Show Trials

When the Haynes farmhouse came into view, Peter broke into a run. He was surprised to find the gate and the double garage doors open. The truck and the family car were both gone. He turned toward the stable, wondering if Charcoal would be out in the lot or in one of the stalls. The big building had sixteen box stalls, eight down each side with a wide aisle between. Peter hurried down the line, looking in at each horse with fast-beating heart.

There was Bourbon's Gold Dust, the Golden American saddle-bred formerly shown by Mr. Haynes but lately taken over by Dodo because she had outgrown Bourbon's Prince, her gaited saddle-bred pony.

There were the three Tennessee Walkers: Red Chief, the Thoroughbred stallion from which Mr. Haynes bred his jumpers; Edna, the fine harness mare; the walk-trot Saddle-bred, Peavine's Chief; the stable's top hunter, Flyer; and a new chestnut Peter had never seen. The rest of the stalls were empty. Disappointed, he turned back to the house. Charcoal must be out in pasture. Yet Dodo had said she was keeping him up at the stable now all the time, schooling him every day, feeding and conditioning him for possible showing later.

No one answered Peter's knock. He set his small suitcase on the porch and sat down disconsolately on the steps. Maybe he had been foolish not to let the Hayneses know. They might even have gone on a trip. While he was trying to figure out what to do next, he heard a cheerful whistling and one of the farm hands swung into view from behind the cow barn. Peter recognized him as the trusted foreman who had been with the Hayneses for years.

"Hi, Jim," he called out.

Jim broke into a smile and hurried toward him. They met in the cleared area by the garage.

"Couldn't hardly believe my eyes!" Jim thrust out a hand. "Good to see you, Pete. The Hayneses and their trainer are all over at Reedsville for the day. Left early this morning."

"Where's Charcoal?" Peter demanded.

Jim looked surprised. "Why . . . with the Hayneses. Didn't Dodo write you? The Reedsville Riding Club is having a practice day in preparation for their horse show and rodeo in June. They had jumps set up over a real course, and Dodo wanted to try your horse out against a little competition. Say! Joe and Red Jones are here to do the milking if I don't get back in time. I'll take my car and drive you over—surprise the

Hayneses. We ought to get there in time to see some of the events. The folks took three horses—yours; a new jumper they got last fall; and Tony, the western parade horse."

"But . . . Jim," Peter almost stuttered, "how could Dodo take a chance on jumping Charcoal yet? I thought we still had to be careful."

"Well now, I'll tell you. Your horse has been coming along wonderfully; but Dodo held back a little in her letters, wanting to surprise you. He hasn't shown a sign of lameness for six weeks now, even with a little jumping every day. Dodo had the local vet check him this week, and he says there's nothing to worry about. Charcoal has lots of stamina and apparently it wasn't a bad case, although it looked like it at first. Good rest and care over the winter did the trick. Well, shall we go? Stow away your luggage in my shack until we get back."

In no time at all they were on the road, bumping along in Jim's ancient Ford. Peter begged for, and got, all the news about the horses at the Haynes farm, the Hayneses themselves, and most of his old friends and neighbors. Riding along through the quiet countryside, he was conscious of a new peace and contentment.

"How does it feel to be back? Maybe you're not so crazy about the city, Pete?"

"No," Peter told him. "I'm not used to such a big school yet."

When they came in sight of the fairgrounds at

Reedsville, there was quite a crowd up in the grandstand watching the practice, enjoying the unusually warm March weather.

"Hey! There's Dodo and Charcoal."

Peter looked eagerly toward the infield where Jim was pointing. He blinked his eyes unbelievingly and looked again. There sat Dodo, resplendent in a new red riding habit, astride a striking jet black horse whose graceful lines bore little resemblance to the rangy, almost awkward Charcoal of the preceding fall. The gelding stood with neck arched and ears alert, watching the crowd and the horses in the ring. The white blaze lent a note of distinction to his well-shaped head. Good feeding, excellent grooming, and loving attention, combined with his own natural growth and development, had transformed the wild unknown into a magnificent piece of horseflesh worthy of any show ring. The thrill of ownership that welled up in Peter was mixed with an odd sense of loss and envy that Dodo, not he, had been able to accomplish the miracle. He tried to choke down the little feeling of jealousy and walked toward the two of them with a big smile. Charcoal seemed nervous, as if the crowds and excitement bothered him.

Dodo saw Peter even before he crossed the track. Her look of surprise gave way to joyful welcome as she waved and motioned him onward. She seemed to be watching him intently. Peter was surprised at her first words. They were not of herself or Charcoal at all.

"I was watching you all the way. You're walking different, not limping a bit. Oh, Peter, I'm so glad! And I'm surprised to see you. How did you manage to come?"

Quickly Peter told her about Dr. Bush's examination and his apparent recovery from the old injury. As he talked, his hands caressed Charcoal's head and neck and his eyes feasted on the new-found beauty of the black horse. The gelding quieted somewhat at his touch but was still restive. He stood a good sixteen hands, and the former coltish gangliness had melted into a well-rounded back and filled-out neck and shoulder muscles. Watching him, Peter was quiet. Dodo flung a stray red curl back from her forehead, then looked at him curiously.

"You've done wonders with him," Peter told her. "Jim said how well he is."

The gelding nuzzled him, and a lump came into Peter's throat. Dodo and Charcoal were so perfect together.

"Peter, we're on next—novice jumper class. I'll have to go. Watch closely now. He's fit, but jittery."

Peter stepped back as she urged Charcoal out onto the track. He leaned across the rail, hardly conscious that Jim had come up beside him.

The foreman noted his shining eyes. "Looks pretty good, doesn't he?"

"I'll say!"

Peter watched Dodo bring Charcoal around and

[113]

head him for the first jump. It seemed as if she too had lost a lot of gangliness over the winter. For the first time he noticed how pretty Dodo was. She gripped the reins tightly, trying to hold the black firmly on the course. He topped the first low jump as if it didn't exist, then shied violently at a sudden movement near the rail. Dodo was almost unseated, but she managed to regain her balance and force him back onto the course.

At the next jump Charcoal slowed almost to a stop. Prepared this time, Dodo stayed firmly in the saddle. She kicked his sides, and Charcoal took the jump almost from a standstill. The crowd gasped. They had expected a refusal, and the actual jump was so effortless it was hard to believe. Peter swallowed. He watched anxiously for any sign of lameness or favoring of the injured leg. The horse was galloping straight and true. Nothing to worry about on that score. The next jump was four feet. The gelding rose to it this time as if he were beginning to enjoy himself. There was still another jump halfway on around the track. It had been set up for those who wanted to try four and a half feet, and it was a drop bar. Peter hoped Dodo wouldn't try it. The horse was going sound. Why tempt their luck? He was intensely relieved when she turned back off the course.

"Thought I wouldn't try him on the higher jump yet," Dodo explained, sliding off and handing the reins to Jim. "He's scared of the crowds and the noise. After all it's his first time out in public. He'll smooth out. Take him back to the truck, Jim, will you? Then we can watch the rest of the trials without worrying about him."

Peter hated to see Charcoal go, but he too was anxious to watch and compare. The next horse out was a blood bay, almost too short-coupled. He took all three jumps easily, but with very little to spare on the four-foot. Then followed in rapid succession three other outside horses . . . and finally the Hayneses' own entry, the new gray mare.

"Dad has high hopes for Gray Girl," Dodo said. "He paid a good price for her as a green prospect last fall, and she's been working out O.K. Watch carefully. I think Willetts, our trainer, plans to try her at four and a half."

"How come you're not riding Gray Girl?" Peter asked.

"That's easy! I've been spending all my time on Charcoal. I haven't had a chance to get used to the mare, or she to me."

The gray was doing a beautiful job. She took all the other jumps and headed for the four-foot-six bars. The onlookers craned their necks. Gray Girl was the first to try it. The mare was well built and well bred and, according to Dodo, had sense and courage. Now it showed in her steady performance. Peter held his breath, hoping she'd make it. There was a shout from

[115]

the crowd. Gray Girl was up and over the final jump. Peter relaxed and turned to Dodo.

"Charcoal could do it too, though. Say, Dodo, could you bring him home in about a month? I can learn to ride a jumper, now that Doc Bush says I'm O.K., and I'd like to enter Charcoal in the novice class at the Civic Horse Show in June. There's our own show at the Academy in May, too, for practice ahead of time. You could come up and ride him in the June show. Will you? It'll be his first real one."

A shadow fell suddenly across Dodo's face. "Yes," she said slowly. "I'll bring him home any time you say." She hesitated. "I'm glad you're going to get to ride him yourself, Peter. Honest, I am. I kind of hoped to enter him in the Reedsville show here. Didn't know just when you'd want to take him back."

Peter noticed the hesitation, the sudden flatness in her tone. So Dodo had really grown to love Charcoal! Well, he wanted to begin to ride his own horse too.

The rest of the visit passed all too quickly. After the trials he went home with the Hayneses in the family car. They all had a good evening around the fireplace, and in the morning Dodo and he had a long ride on Bourbon's Prince, her old Saddle-bred pony, and Charcoal. The whole family took Peter to the bus station early Sunday afternoon, waiting while he stopped to say goodbye to Dr. Bush.

All the way back to the city Peter pondered the problem of what to do about Charcoal. Riding with

Dodo, he had thrilled to the surge of power in the black gelding, the feel of his sensitive, responsive mouth, and his easy, effortless gaits. He could imagine how it would feel to be sailing over the jumps, and his fingers itched to hold the reins and be at it. But could he learn to handle a jumper in time for the season's shows? Would it be fair to Charcoal to take him away from Dodo and give him a green rider over the jumps? And what about Dodo herself?

Back home, Peter told his folks the good news from the doctor and all about his plans to bring Charcoal back in April. Then he phoned Dick Stearns, who had taken over a service station.

"How about coming out once or twice to get me started? I'll pay you. Dad's no jumping teacher, as you know. If I'm to do justice to Charcoal later, I've got to learn to ride a jumper right. Dad isn't very crazy about the idea. Thinks I'll spend so much time on this I won't help him much, but he says I can use our gentle old veteran jumper, White Eagle, to learn on. How about it?"

"Sure I'll come. But I never know when I get my afternoon off till the last minute. I'll have to let you know. But you're not paying me anything. Believe me, I'll be glad of an excuse to be around there again. I miss the horses plenty, and being valet to a lot of gas buggies doesn't satisfy me. Too bad there aren't more riding academies in this area that specialize in jumping. I might have gotten another teaching job."

From then on, it was a steady grind for Peter. Up early to do the paper route; the day at school, an hour and a half helping with the stable work; dinner; twice a week an evening beginner's class of riders to teach, and two classes on the week ends. Studying was sandwiched in between. There was no time for recreation and scarcely time to keep up correspondence with Dodo, although Peter was more anxious than ever to know how Charcoal was progressing. Dick came twice that first week and gave him lessons; after that he came once every week or two. He steadfastly refused to take any pay for his help; but he would often jump White Eagle or one of the other horses when Peter was through, just to keep in the swing of things.

Starting with very low jumps and working up gradually, Peter found it fairly easy. In fact, jumping wasn't half as exciting as he'd imagined it; but he attributed that to the fact that White Eagle, although safe and consistent, was hard-gaited on the straightaway, unresponsive and hard-mouthed. He knew how to jump and he practically took the bit in his teeth and went over in his own way, with no help from his rider. Peter felt like a passenger rather than a pilot. He began to long for Charcoal's lightness of movement, responsive, soft mouth, and the sense of sharing an adventure the black always brought him. He was tickled to death when the days finally rolled by and it was just two more weeks till Charcoal would be coming home.

CHAPTER XII

Disappointment

April was at its very best the Saturday that Charcoal arrived. Peter had wanted to see the expression on his father's face when the gelding was first unloaded; but when the Haynes car and trailer finally rolled into the driveway about two o'clock, John Morgan was out with a group of riders. Dodo waved at Peter from the car, jumped out, and stood ready to help before the car came to a stop.

"How is he?" Peter asked eagerly. Then he suddenly remembered his manners. He felt foolish and grinned at Dodo, who was looking at him understandingly. "I mean, how are both of *you?*" He turned toward Mr. Haynes as the latter got out of the car.

"Fine! Fine!" Mr. Haynes shook hands and then reached for the tail gate. "Let's unload and then look up your folks, Pete. I expect your horse is mighty tired after his long ride."

Charcoal backed down so quietly Peter could hardly

believe he was the same horse that had caused them so much trailer trouble before.

Dodo laughed at his surprise. "We've been drilling him on trailer etiquette. After all, if he's going to be a show horse, he's got to be a good traveler. He learned fast."

Again Peter felt a little twinge of jealousy, although he was grateful to the Hayneses and said so. He took the lead rope and led the black gelding proudly in through the big door of the stable section.

Bob, the stableman, met him halfway down the row of stalls and stopped to stare. "Man! Oh, man! That wild broomtail of yours from the hills has turned into a real beauty. If he can jump as pretty as he looks, some of the veterans around here better look to their laurels."

Peter glowed with pride. He could hardly wait to show the gelding to his father. While Mr. Haynes and Dodo visited with his mother in the house, he stayed in the stall with Charcoal, stroking his sleek neck and velvety muzzle. Every now and then he went to the door to see if there was any sign of his father. It seemed very important that John Morgan be surprised and pleased at the colt's development.

The telephone rang suddenly. Bob went to answer. He listened a moment, then called Peter excitedly.

"Hey, Pete, come quick. It's your Dad!"

There was urgency in Bob's tone, and he looked scared as he handed over the receiver.

John Morgan's voice came over the wire in clipped, quick sentences. "Pete, you and your mother and Bob come to Linden Road and Chester immediately. There's been an accident, and we've four riderless horses to get back to the stable. You and Bob can each ride one and lead one. Don't ask questions now. Just get going! Tell your mother it's one of the girls."

Peter hung up the phone and dashed to the house. He burst in on the Hayneses and his mother with the message.

Mrs. Morgan paled. "How bad is it? Who's hurt?"

"I don't know. Get your coat!"

"We'll take our car and trailer," Mr. Haynes interrupted, starting toward the door. "Saves getting your car out of the garage, and one of the horses can be brought back in it. That way Bob can stay here. *Someone* should."

The Morgans and Dodo followed Mr. Haynes to the big Buick and piled in. Peter directed him to Linden Road and Chester, a mile or so away. Fear welled up in his thoat so that it felt dry and raw. He knew how worried and harassed his father was already. He kept hoping the accident wasn't serious, and it seemed to take ages to drive the short distance. They found only a young man and two frightened girls holding the four horses. One of the girls was crying. Peter took her horse.

"What on earth happened?"

"He ran away," she sobbed. "A car full of kids acting smart came up close and honked suddenly. The horse started running and slipped on the pavement. Peg was pinned underneath. The horse got right up, but she just lay there. It was awful. Mr. Morgan went with the ambulance to take her to the hospital. He's going to telephone our folks to come get us. We wouldn't ride back to the stable for anything."

"I just happened along and saw they needed help," the young man added. "Your father asked if I'd stay here and take charge of the horses till the girls' people came. He was pretty upset. I'll go along now if you have no further need of me." He handed Dodo the reins of the two horses he was holding.

Peter thanked him. He had unconsciously assumed command of the situation in his father's absence.

"I'll ride one horse. Dodo can ride another, and we'll take turns leading one of the other two. The horse that fell better go in the trailer, Mr. Haynes. He's skinned up, and probably still so scared he'd be sort of spooky to ride. Mother, you and Mr. Haynes will have to stay with the girls till their folks come; then bring the last horse. We'll start ahead. You'll probably catch up with us anyway."

"Well," Dodo sighed as they started slowly along the graveled shoulder of the paved highway, "I had hoped we'd get to take a ride together this afternoon, but I didn't expect it to be like this."

"I should say not," Peter told her glumly. "Poor Dad!"

"How about the girl that got hurt?"

"Well, I'm sorry for her too," Peter admitted, "but Dad has signs up all over the stable, 'Not responsible for accidents to riders.' It's not his fault that crazy drivers sometimes have no consideration for people on horseback. And it sure did spoil Charcoal's home-coming."

"Peter, I'm ashamed of you." Dodo's voice was scolding. "What if I had been the one hurt?"

Peter had a queer feeling all of a sudden. "I wouldn't like that," he said sheepishly. "Guess you're right. I should be thinking about Peg. I hope she isn't hurt bad."

Back at the Academy the four of them waited anxiously for word from John Morgan. Finally he phoned from the hospital to say the girl had broken a leg, but the doctor and her folks were there and he'd soon be home. They were not to come for him. He'd get a taxi just outside the hospital.

When he finally came in, he looked pale and drawn. "Well, that's that," he said unhappily. "Peg's parents blame me, and the other two girls swear they'll never ride again. This short of thing could happen to anyone, but it's bad publicity. Between seeing my horses abused by careless riders and my riders hurt by careless drivers, I'm about ready to give up the Academy.'

Mrs. Morgan went over and put her arm around

him. "John, it wasn't your fault. Try not to worry."

"That's a bad route along that highway," John Morgan continued broodingly. "But it's getting so built up around here that there's no place to ride any more without hitting pavement."

"I know just what you mean," Mr. Haynes said decidedly. "I prefer the open country."

Finally John Morgan roused from his apathy. "I'm glad to see you folks, even if I don't act like it. I suppose you brought the boy's horse."

"Yes." Dodo's voice was eager. "Wouldn't you like to see him?"

"All right." John Morgan spoke without enthusiasm, but he followed them out to the stable. His sober gray eyes inspected the gelding, lighting up briefly in spite of his mood. Peter, watching him closely, knew that he was impressed, but all he said was, "How's the tendon?"

"Fine!" Mr. Haynes' voice was proud. "Dodo worked hard with Charcoal, John. I'd really like—" Suddenly he caught himself, stopped, and changed the subject. "I'd like to see him at his first show."

After the Hayneses had started home, Peter went back to the black gelding. He led him out and studied him intently, loving the slim grace and elegance of the trim five-year-old.

"Wild horse, me eye," Bob exclaimed, coming up behind him. "That horse is bred in the royal, no matter where he came from. On one side or the other there's quality—maybe on both."

Peter glowed. He was itching to ride Charcoal, maybe test him over a low jump or two; but he wouldn't try it after the long trailer trip. Tomorrow would be soon enough.

Too excited to sleep much, Peter arose on Sunday tired but determined to ride Charcoal. He saddled the gelding right after breakfast and took him into the inside ring, where he had set up a course of three- and four-foot jumps. He tried to remember everything Dick had taught him about the special techniques of jumping. But being on solid, gentle old White Eagle was entirely different from being on the buoyant, spirited young gelding. Charcoal felt very good indeed. He was restive and anxious to be at the jumps, straining at the bit and prancing sideways.

Peter suddenly felt all the confidence ooze out of him. Charcoal needed wisdom and experience, a steadying hand, not the elementary knowledge and uncertain hand of a beginner like himself. The horse seemed to sense his lack of confidence and shook his head impatiently. Peter loosed the reins and let him go. The old habit of clinging to the saddle rose up from the days of his lameness. He clutched at the pommel, forgetting his old handhold was no longer there. Charcoal rose sloppily on the first low jump.

Peter did not have him collected properly, and he knew it. The seat, the balance, even the way of holding the reins—all were different in jumping.

He decided to just stick on and let Charcoal get over the jumps as best he could. He missed the steady helpfulness of old White Eagle. He wasn't ready for Charcoal yet . . . no use fooling himself. The gelding slowed down and lost interest in the job at hand. He cleared the jumps by only a few inches, with a minimum of effort and more heavily each time. Peter turned him out of the course and sighed wearily. The great moment he had waited for so long was a bitter disappointment. He knew the fault was not Charcoal's. Yet something was decidedly wrong. With a heavy heart Peter put the black gelding back in his stall.

CHAPTER XIII

Stalemate

Charcoal seemed to respond to him about as well as ever when not asked to jump. But, try as he might, Peter could not get the black to clear the bars with any degree of enthusiasm. Doggedly he saddled up every day and put the horse through his paces for at least twenty minutes; but he didn't particularly enjoy it, and Charcoal didn't act as if he did either.

"What's the matter with him?" Peter finally begged Dick in desperation. The trainer had come out the second Sunday after Charcoal was back, in response to the boy's frantic plea for help. Dick's only response to the question was to send them back over the jumps while he watched closely. When Peter once more drew up in front of him, he came down and stood looking up at his friend.

"Pete, tell me the truth. Do you yourself honestly like jumping? I wondered all the time I was trying to teach you, but didn't want to arouse any doubts in your mind if you really were happier about it than it seemed."

Peter swallowed and looked away. He dreaded the question; but, knowing Dick, he had had a hunch it would come.

"No, I'm afraid I don't . . . not as much as straight riding. I always thought I would, so I can't figure out why. Maybe it's because Charcoal just doesn't give for me. I'm not afraid."

Dick nodded his head knowingly. "I guessed as much from watching you. You're not relaxed and happy, and the horse knows it. How can you expect him to put his heart into it when you don't? Why don't you quit trying if you feel like that?"

Peter gripped the reins a little harder. A stubborn look came into his eyes. "Maybe he'll jump better for me later. I want Charcoal to be good. I want him to be the best jumper in these parts."

"Why?" Dick asked bluntly. "To prove that you were right and your father and some of the others were wrong?"

Peter faced up to it. "That's partly it. But it's mostly because of Charcoal. You said yourself he was born to jump. He's my responsibility. You remember how I was his favorite before. He wouldn't even perform as well for you. Now I've lost him somehow."

"Let me take him around once," Dick suggested. "It may be just because he feels you aren't quite sure of yourself yet. The reins are just like telegraph wires to a horse."

Peter gladly relinquished the saddle. He watched eagerly as Dick piloted the black expertly over every jump. Charcoal made each one easily, but with no particular brilliance and nothing to spare.

"He's only half trying," Dick called out. "How about trying five feet? Maybe he's bored because we haven't given him any real challenge. Has his leg showed any sign of lameness since he came back?"

"No. Go ahead."

Dick raised the bars, and Peter watched tensely as the black headed for the jump. Charcoal took off gracefully, but Peter choked back an involuntary cry. He'd never make it. There hadn't been quite enough drive in those hind legs. Even as he listened for the sharp crack of hoofs striking the bar, he heard a triumphant shout from Dick and saw that the gelding had cleared it by the fraction of an inch. Charcoal could have done better, but at least he hadn't faulted.

Dick came round again and dismounted. He stroked Charcoal gently between the eyes. "He's a horse with a single love, Pete, and it isn't you. He likes you; but it's Dodo he's given his heart to now, and I'm afraid you'll just have to face it. I'm not a hundred per cent sure of this; but once I've seen her jump him, I'll know."

Peter hated hearing it put into words. He mounted

the black and gathered up the reins almost fiercely. "Won't he forget Dodo in time?"

"I doubt it." Dick shook his head. "But don't give up yet. Keep trying. Maybe as you learn more about jumping, you two will get along better. Come on. I'll give you a few more pointers. Sorry I can't come oftener."

Peter wrote a short note to Dodo saying that he was jumping Charcoal every day and that he had cleared five feet. It had to be brief because he couldn't say more without saying too much, and he didn't want to admit apparent failure.

Peg's folks had not made any trouble over the accident, but four or five of the regular riders dropped out because their parents thought the bridle trails were too dangerous. John Morgan seemed cast into an even deeper gloom than usual. Peter did his best to keep out of his way, helping regularly with the work but being careful not to bring Charcoal too much to his attention. He was afraid his father would again bring up the idea of renting him to the better jumping students.

Early in June, Peter entered the black in the novice-jumping class at the Civic Horse Show. He had skipped their own Academy show in May, because he knew he wasn't ready to ride and he hated to ask Dodo to come so far for such a small show. The Civic Show was to be the last week in the month, so practice sessions became doubly important. The gelding seemed steadier, but Peter wished there were some way to accustom him to crowds and music beforehand. As they became more used to each other, boy and horse reached a sort of unspoken agreement; but there was still something missing. Charcoal was holding back just enough for Peter to detect a difference.

The gelding was getting all the exercise he needed from the daily jumping workout, so when Peter wanted to ride just for relaxation he began taking Star out again. He still had his paper route, and every morning the stallion and he had their visit while covering it; but there were other times when he felt the need of Star's smoothness and dependability. Temperamental and moody with others, he was always gentle and affectionate with Peter. There was a fascination about Charcoal, an irresistible something that would not let Peter stop trying to win his affection; but he never felt the same solid comfort and full comradeship that he felt with Star.

Peter had practically promised Dodo she could ride the black gelding at his first show. Yet he couldn't quite bring himself to write and remind her. Instead he stubbornly schooled the black himself every chance he got.

Dodo wrote that they were coming up for the Civic Show with several horses, but she didn't ask to ride Charcoal nor remind Peter of his promise. The Academy had to use the trailer for its own entries, so Jerry helped haul Charcoal to the grounds when the big day finally arrived. Peter was so nervous he could hardly unload the gelding. He knew he was hurting the black's chances, yet he wanted desperately to have the thrill of riding his own horse—the horse he had broken himself and helped to train.

CHAPTER XIV

First Show and a Double

It would be some time before Charcoal's jumping class was called. Peter was grateful for the chance to steady himself and think out his problem.

He tied the gelding to the side of the truck and with Jerry walked over to the rail below the grandstand to watch the other classes. The three-gaited, 15.2 hands and under, came first, and then a five-gaited division. Peter was tremendously interested in both of them, because his father was essentially a gaited-horse trainer and these were the kind of classes he loved and understood. As he watched the beautiful flashing action, he wondered if he were not really more interested in working with gaited horses and Tennessee Walkers than with jumpers. Yet it was too soon to tell, for he hadn't actually ridden a jumper in a real show.

After the gaited classes came a hunter event, in which conformation would be scored along with performance. Here the registered Thoroughbreds stood the best chance as a rule, for their good breeding showed up in fine body lines and sensitive, well-formed heads. Peter watched intently as the first entry made the course with beautiful timing and precision. As the horse left the ring, he glanced back toward the truck to be sure Charcoal was all right; and when he brought his eyes back to the entrance gate, his jaw dropped open in bewilderment. Peter blinked. He had just seen Charcoal tied to the truck, right where he had left him; yet there was Charcoal coming onto the track!

In utter amazement he studied the black horse trotting on. In shape, markings, movement, and expression he was an identical twin to Charcoal. Searching scrutiny revealed only one minor difference. The newcomer was a trifle larger and heavier than the gelding, a little more fully developed. Peter turned to Jerry, who was staring at the hunter entry with the same fascinated wonder.

"Jumping Jehoshaphat!" Jerry said. "They're as alike as two peas. Look at him, boy! He even moves like Charcoal, with that same light, springy action, that same proud bearing of the head and neck. Here, let's see who he is—who owns him."

Peter and Jerry turned their programs to Class 3 almost simultaneously, but Peter was the first to speak.

"Number Two. He's Black Beau the Third, owned by Wilson Parks of Yakima, Washington."

"We'll find this Parks right after that horse comes

off. I'll wager you any money your Charcoal is related in some way to Black Beau, Peter. My boy, I have the feeling we're on the track of something big."

Peter could scarcely control his impatience till the black Thoroughbred finished the course, although his excitement mounted as the horse rose magnificently to each jump and left the ring with a faultless score.

"Come on," Jerry directed.

He skirted the outside of the course and hurried into the infield, half running. Peter was right on his heels. He caught up with Jerry just as the latter reached Black Beau and spoke to the clean-cut, middle-aged sportsman on his back.

"Does this horse belong to you?"

"Sure does. Why do you ask?"

Peter couldn't keep still. "That's why!" He pointed across the track to where Jerry's truck and Charcoal were clearly in evidence.

Black Beau's owner stared. "I see," he said quietly. "I'll have to strip Beau and lead him out afterward for the conformation judging, or I may be called back for a jump-off; but there are five more entries in this class. I'm going over to see that horse!"

Getting off, he handed the Thoroughbred's reins to a nearby friend.

"My name is Parks—Wilson Parks. Run a Hereford ranch up near Yakima, but show horses are my hobby. I usually show mainly in Washington. This is a fare-well performance for Black Beau. The old boy's fifteen and I'm retiring him to stud. He's been a wonder in jumping circles for a good many years now."

Jerry introduced himself and Peter as they skirted the course and crossed the track. He finished explaining about Charcoal and how he had come to them from the wild herd.

The genial rancher studied Charcoal from every angle, exclaiming under his breath. "When was it you got this fellow? And about how old was he?"

"It was a little less than two years ago and, as near as we could tell from his teeth and general development, he was about three then," Jerry answered.

"That explains it!" Mr. Parks struck a clenched fist into the palm of his other hand. "As you know, my horse is a stallion. Not quite six years ago I was taking him and another horse to a show here in Portland, pulling the trailer behind my car. As I was coming through one of the most deserted and barren parts of the Horse Heaven Hills, where the highway winds through one of those narrow canyons, a truck rammed into me. I blacked out—was hurt pretty bad, in fact—and woke up in a hospital.

"They told me the other horse had been badly hurt and had to be destroyed, but Black Beau had gotten away, apparently unhurt, and taken to the hills. The truck driver was too concerned about me to bother with him—just brought me on into town. When my men went out to look for Beau he couldn't be found. He had joined a wild herd, and it was three months before I got out of the hospital and was able to search for him.

"He's a favorite of mine, wonderful blood lines and one of the best jumpers in the Northwest. I was determined to find him; and after ten days of solid searching on horseback with five men, we spotted him. He didn't want to leave the band of wild mares he had collected, but we finally cornered and roped him. He must have sired several pretty fine colts during that time, for I noticed two or three mares of above-average quality in his band—probably ranch horses of good breeding turned out on the summer range and not found again in the fall. I'll bet my bottom dollar your horse here is a colt of Beau's out of one of those better mares. Of course there's no way to prove it positively, but the evidence is there in his looks. Too bad you had him gelded. He looks more like old Beau than any of the colts I *know* are his. How does your horse perform?"

"He jumped six feet once," Peter explained proudly. "And he was awfully easy to break and train. I knew he wasn't any common broomtail."

"You've got a wonderful horse here, son, if he's by my stud. Hang on to him. Well, I've got to get back to the old boy himself. If you ever want to part with this gelding, let me know. He may follow in his sire's footsteps as a jumper. Anyway I'd buy him just to keep reminded of Old Beau after he's gone."

Peter sighed. "I'm sure glad we ran into you, Mr.

Parks. I know we can't prove it, but I'm sure too that Charcoal is Black Beau's son. It would account for so many things about him that have kept us guessing. I hope he does well today. Then you can see for yourself."

Mr. Parks hastily scribbled on a card and handed it to Peter. "Here's my name and address. Keep me informed about your horse's progress if I don't see you around at the shows. Goodbye!"

Peter lost all interest in the progress of the show. Leaving Jerry in charge of Charcoal, he rushed out to find his father and tell him the good news. Then he ran into Dodo, dressed in her riding clothes. There wasn't time to tell her the whole story, because Charcoal's class was next; but he blurted out the essential parts, watching her face light up with incredulous joy. The way she looked first at him and then at Charcoal, there was only one thing for Peter to do. Charcoal simply *had* to have the best possible chance to prove himself now. And that meant the best possible rider.

He turned away from Dodo, hiding his thoughts, thinking fast. He busied himself saddling and bridling the gelding, while Dodo leaned against the trailer and idly slapped her boot with her riding crop. She didn't say a word. Up in the stands seven people were waiting and watching for Peter and Charcoal—including Dr. Bush, who had come with the Hayneses and stopped for a quick physical checkup on Peter before

coming on to the show grounds. Peter suspected that
had been planned between his folks and the doctor,
and he was relieved when his old friend slapped him
on the back and said it was all right to ride. The
Hayneses hadn't stopped—said they had to go on and
settle-in their horses. Peter had thought it strange at
the time.

The more he thought about the home folks sitting
up there and the faith they had in him, the more
Peter realized he couldn't go through with it. He led
Charcoal over and handed the reins to Dodo, feeling
a queer mixture of bitter disappointment and marked
relief.

"Here," he said. "You ride him. He'll do better for
you, and I want him to win. Anyway I promised you
this first real show."

They were announcing the class. There was no time
to argue. Flashing him an all-embracing look of surprise and gratitude, Dodo mounted and rode to the
arena. The folks in the grandstand were surprised
when Peter slipped into the seat reserved for Dodo,
but his eyes were riveted on the gate and the horses
awaiting their turn. Charcoal fretted impatiently.
Dodo's lips were moving, and she was stroking his
neck in an effort to soothe him.

Cold sweat broke out on Peter's forehead. Had he
been a fool to change his mind at the last minute?
Maybe Charcoal wouldn't do any better for Dodo
after all. But at least he had kept his promise.

"How come?" Hank asked him audibly. "Weren't scared out, were you?"

"No!" Peter turned away disgustedly. He'd never be able to make Hank understand, but the rest of them would.

He had to watch five horses go over the course before Charcoal's number was finally announced. Dodo took a firm grip on the reins and urged the gelding through the gate. To hold him tight enough to keep him from running off the course or around the jump, yet at the same time to give him enough freedom for a proper takeoff . . . that was the problem. A fine line of balance lay between the two. Peter held his breath and saw the black rise to the first jump. They were over it, in the clear, and down without mishap. Dodo seemed to settle more closely into the saddle and lean forward.

The second jump was just ahead. Charcoal rose with a new surge of power and landed cleanly. Dodo was thrown a trifle off balance but made a quick recovery. Peter could sense a striking change of attitude in the black. Charcoal was jumping on his own now—for the fun of it. Dodo gave the horse his head on the next barrier, and he jumped high and handsome. He left a good margin for the crowd to gasp over; and when he came back to the entrance gate with a clean record, Peter knew he stood high on the list—just how high he wasn't sure until the judges added up their score pads and called Charcoal out for the blue. Having done his duty and vindicated Peter's faith, the black gelding pranced once around the ring like a parade horse, shying, tossing his head, acting as silly as if he had not jumped as steadily as a veteran.

Peter went straight down to Dodo—the first to reach her with congratulations. Some of the others came and shook his hand, but Peter had eyes only for one face—his father's.

John Morgan smiled as if he understood the reason. "You've got a good horse," he said. "And it was decent of you to let Dodo ride."

That was all, but it was enough. Dodo slipped off, beaming, and handed Peter the reins. She hurried off to find her parents. Peter looked at Charcoal and saw how the gelding's eyes followed Dodo back toward the stands. There was wistfulness and sudden respect in his voice as he stroked the gelding's sweaty neck.

"It's O.K.," he told the black. "She deserved it, and I know you can't help liking her more than me."

Charcoal showed twice more that summer. "Don't put him in too many shows," Dick cautioned. "Remember he's young yet, as jumpers go, and he may have some slight weakness in that injured tendon. Take no chances of crippling him again."

At the second show, Peter rode. He did his best, but the gelding was inconsistent and came out with a third-place ribbon. At the final show, Peter insisted that Dodo ride again. Charcoal went all out for her with a joyous abandon and brought home another blue. Peter was both happy and sad. He still wanted to get the best from Charcoal himself, but he was triumphant over the results of that first season.

When Dodo informed him she was going to stay in the city next year and live with her aunt so she could go to a city high school, he was surprised and jubilant.

"Wish your aunt lived in our part of town, so we'd get to go to the same school," he said, and meant it.

"I do too." Dodo's voice was rueful. "I won't have any horse here, and I'll miss them all terribly. I hope you'll let me ride Charcoal often."

Too happy in Charcoal's new ascendancy to feel any jealousy, Peter assured her it would be O.K. He smiled down at her, realizing suddenly how much taller he had grown in the past year.

"We'll ride together every week end if you'll come over. After all I still have Star."

CHAPTER XV

The Storm

After school started in the fall, life for Peter settled more or less into a routine. The paper route, school, exercising Charcoal, and the stable work took up all of his week-day time. He looked forward to the week ends; for in spite of helping with the beginning riders, he had time to catch up with things, ride with Dodo, and even go to a movie or do some sketching. Besides, every Saturday he gave both Star and Charcoal a thorough grooming till their black coats shone like satin.

Fall and winter business fell off at the Academy, and again it seemed that John Morgan would be unable to meet his payment on time. The boarding horses became doubly important as the one regular source of income that could be counted on. But there was no more stall room inside the big barn. Hating to turn down new boarders, Peter's father sold three of the rent horses to make room, but soon every stall within the stable proper was full again. Late in November he called Peter aside. He had been talking to a man Peter had never seen before, and his face was drawn and worried.

"Pete, I hate like everything to do it, but this gentleman has had a registered American Saddle-bred show horse shipped up from California and wants to board him with us. There's only one stall left I could give him—Charcoal's. We'll have to move your gelding into the outside shed where he was when he first came."

Peter stared at him in amazement. "But, Dad, it's just a shell, full of knotholes and cracks. The wind whistles through the walls as if they were paper, and the roof leaks. The floor's just dirt. Charcoal's soft now from being inside and blanketed, not tough like when he first came. He's proved himself, and he deserves a good stall. Couldn't you move one of the other horses out there, instead, to make room for the new boarder?"

John Morgan's jaw tightened. His voice was hard. "Peter, you know we can't put one rent horse way out there away from the others and expect the stableman to take the extra trouble to go out there to feed and water every day and to get the horse when he's needed. Heaven's knows Bob works hard enough as it is. I won't add to his work. You know how important every cent is to us right now. Why don't you cooperate for a change?"

"For a change?" Peter echoed. "What *have* I been doing for the past year or so?" His voice was hurt and angry. "You know I've been helping you right along, with the stable work and teaching too."

"Your work just about pays for Charcoal's keep. Star earns his way with his stud fees. Now let's hear no more about it. Your horse is a luxury item, and he'll just have to fit in where I can put him. As for the roof, I'll get you some shingles and you can mend it. But Charcoal's not that delicate. He was born and raised on the open range. Basically he's a broomtail, any way you look at it."

Charcoal was put in the old shed the following Saturday. He showed his displeasure at being alone again by kicking the flimsy walls disdainfully, although not as vigorously as he had before.

Dodo was almost as disgusted about the turn of events as Peter.

"I can't understand it," she said surprisedly. "There must have been *some* other way to fix things. Charcoal won't be happy, and I'll bet he won't jump nearly as well. Your Dad sure hasn't been himself lately, Peter. I think this business is getting him down."

"He's worried," Peter pointed out defensively. "Mostly about the next payment on the stable."

"My Dad could lend him the money." Dodo spoke thoughtfully. "He'd be glad to. I'll tip Dad off."

"Don't you dare! Dad would have a fit about my telling you. He doesn't like to ask help from anyone."

Dodo shrugged her shoulders. "O.K. It's your worry.

But I sure hate to see Charcoal stuck way out here, after we've worked so hard to get him well. If he catches cold, it might affect that tendon again. Well, I guess we can't do anything about it. Let's go riding."

Peter felt so sorry for Charcoal and was so worried over what he might do that he spent even more time hovering over him. He patched the roof, kept the stall scrupulously clean, adjusted his blanket several times a day, and reinforced every board that cracked under the onslaught of the black's hoofs. After one particularly vicious kick, he surveyed Charcoal ruefully.

"I guess you've got a wild streak in you yet. When you're mad, it sure comes out with a vengeance."

Peter awakened suddenly from a deep sleep. The wind was pounding against his bedroom wall with terrific intensity, and rain lashed at the windows in great driving sheets. Damp cold, fog, and rain had settled down on the city and its surroundings several weeks before, punctuated only occasionally by a sunny day with frost. There had been minor storms, but this was almost a hurricane. Peter sprang out of bed and looked toward the stable. Dimly he could see the flicker of lights through the lashing rain.

Charcoal would be terrified. There were several big trees near the shed, some of them towering over it. The eerie howling, the thump of the branches pounding against the building, and his loneliness would combine to set the high-strung gelding wild.

Peter got into his jeans and shoes and flung on his shirt. He took time to snatch his jacket from the closet; then he ran outside, pulling it on as he went. The wind caught him full force as he left the shelter of the porch, almost flinging him against the side of the house. He could hear the crash of falling branches, and all kinds of objects came rolling across the open area in front of the stable as if impelled by a giant hand. Avoiding them as best he could, Peter fought his way across the cleared space to the old shed that housed Charcoal. It was not until he was almost up to it that he saw to his horror that the door was wide open, banging back and forth on its hinges with a succession of sharp crashes. There was a big gash in the roof where a huge branch had fallen and punctured the rotten shingles.

Although he knew it was useless, Peter peered inside. It was very black, but he could see no dark shadow in the stall. He stood absolutely still, hoping against hope, listening and watching for some movement, calling to Charcoal again and again. He wished he had thought to bring a flashlight. But there was no doubt of it, the stall was empty! He felt around hopelessly. Remembering the other time Charcoal had gotten loose, Peter's heart felt leaden. In the dark and storm, search was almost useless; but the gelding might have tried to go back to his old stall. Hugging the shelter of the building, Peter plunged toward the big back doors of the stable. He stumbled over a heap of material blown against the wall. As he picked it up to throw aside, he felt buckles and straps. Even as he dragged it into the light from a window, he knew that it was Charcoal's blanket. Mud-stained and badly torn, it must have slipped down; and the horse had kicked himself free of it.

Peter went on all the way around the big building. Everything loose in the countryside seemed to be whirling past him. A falling branch almost grazed his head; a barrel rolling down the slope came straight for him, emerging out of the darkness just in time for him to dodge. Peter knew there was no use to ask his father and the stableman to help. They had their hands full quieting the horses inside and watching the building for possible damage. He would have to go it alone. The short jacket he wore, although rain-repellent, was poor protection against the cold and deluge. The lower part of his body was already soaked, and the dampness was beginning to come through on his shoulders. Rain plastered his hair and ran in rivulets down his face. If only he'd had sense enough to grab a cap!

Driven by a sort of desperation at the thought of abandoning Charcoal to the fury of the storm, Peter picked his way along the paddock fence, over familiar trails, twice across to the highway, almost a mile down through the woods, calling the gelding by name.

Weak, almost crying with chagrin, Peter came back to the warmth of the house after more than an hour of vain searching. His feet were cold, wet, and covered with mud. His clothes were soaked; he was chilled clean through and twice he had fallen over obstacles blown across the path, until his hands were skinned and raw with cold.

His mother met him anxiously at the door as he stumbled inside. "Where on earth have you been? I went to your room about half an hour ago, wondering how you could sleep through all this din. When I saw you were gone, I figured you were out with the men in the stable. But you're half drowned. Where *were* you?"

"Looking for Charcoal," Peter muttered. "He's gone again. I couldn't find a trace of him. Please ask Dad to look some more."

"We'll find him in the morning. Get those wet clothes off this minute! There's hot coffee on the stove, and I want you straight in bed. I'll bring you a hot drink and a hot-water bottle. You're shaking so hard your teeth are rattling."

Peter realized she was right. Back in the heated room, he had begun to chill violently. He had been too worried to think about his own condition; now too tired and miserable to argue, he did as his mother suggested. In bed, with plenty of covers and warmth, Peter still continued to shake with cold. The wind had died down a little and the rain had settled to a steady drizzle, but Peter kept trying to figure out where Charcoal might have gone. He hoped desperately the gelding was somewhere near, for by now the Academy should have become home to him. He wanted very much to stay awake, get thoroughly warm, and then go out to look some more; but he was so exhausted that as the warmth stole over him he fell asleep.

CHAPTER XVI

Sickness

It seemed hours later when Peter awakened. His head ached furiously. He threw off the covers and stumbled sleepily to the bedroom window. It was morning. The rain was still falling in a monotonous drizzle, and everything outside looked drenched and soggy gray.

Charcoal! Where was he? Had he come through the storm unhurt? Peter grabbed his clothes and skinned into them faster than he ever had before, although his joints ached, his throat burned, and his head was splitting. The wind had died down, and his father was in the kitchen making coffee. He looked up as Peter barged in.

"Hey! Where's Charcoal? Did he come home?"

"Yes." John Morgan put a finger to his lips. "Quiet! Your mother's trying to sleep after being awake nearly all night. Your horse was waiting outside the big barn at daylight to get back into his old stall. I turned him into the inside ring."

"Is he all right?"

"Yes, but you sound as if *you've* caught cold. Better go back to bed. We'll be having a late breakfast."

"I'm going out to Charcoal," Peter insisted.

He wanted to reassure himself by seeing and touching the gelding. He found him standing rather dejectedly in the big cold ring, head low. No one had thought to put on another blanket, so Peter hunted out an old one from the Academy supply and buckled it on snugly. Charcoal raised his head and nickered softly when Peter walked away. There was a strangeness about him Peter didn't like, a new sense of dependence and distress.

He went back to bed and tried to sleep, but he kept worrying about where his father would put the gelding now. The outside shed was a wreck. It would need a new roof, and Heaven alone knew how it was to be paid for. Loose horses could not be left in the ring when there were classes or practice. Relief at Charcoal's being safe at home mingled with worry over the future until Peter's mind became so confused he gave up trying to think and dozed off again.

When his mother called him, it was nearly noon. Thunderstruck to find he had slept so long, Peter dressed and ate a hasty brunch. He hurried to the big ring, but Charcoal had disappeared. On his way out to look for him, he saw Bob, his father, and another man in earnest consultation at the door of one of the largest box stalls. With a sense of foreboding, he came up behind them and looked in. There stood Charcoal, his eyes lusterless, his legs braced, and his body shaking at intervals as if from a violent chill, although he still wore the old blanket.

Peter clung to the door. The knuckles of his hands stood out white and strained against the brown skin. His tongue felt harsh and dry. His voice sank almost to a whisper.

"What's the matter? I thought he was all right."

The third man turned. Peter recognized Dr. Gray, the kindly veterinary who had treated Charcoal's injured tendon. He put a hand on Peter's shoulder.

"Take it easy, son. Your horse *seemed* all right when your father told you that. This has come on in the last few hours. He's taken cold, and it's showing signs of possible pneumonia. Keep him well blanketed, out of draughts, and rub and bandage his legs every few hours. Call me at once if he develops a cough, a nasal discharge, or complete loss of appetite. I'll check again tomorrow even if I don't hear from you. Remember to keep plenty of fresh, cool water available for him all the time."

Peter opened the stall door and went in. He threw his arms around the gelding and pressed his face tight against his mane so his father would not see the anger and bitterness welling up in him. His hands caressed Charcoal's head and neck. They were hot to his touch and moist with sweat in spite of the chills which continued to shake the gelding's body.

[153]

"You can't get pneumonia," Peter muttered under his breath. "You just *can't*!" "It's my fault—not staying out till I found you."

"If he hadn't been so softened up with blankets and warm stalls till he had no proper winter coat, the exposure never would have bothered him," Bob remarked. "Don't you worry, Pete. He's basically tough. Doc Gray and all of us pulling together will have him snapped out of this in no time. Stay with him, boy. A horse that knows people is frightened and lonely when he's sick."

"You don't have to tell me." Peter swallowed. "I won't leave him a minute except to eat." He went out, got a folding camp stool from the tack room, and set it inside the stall near Charcoal's head. He got down on his knees and rubbed the black's cold legs vigorously till they felt warm to the touch. Then he wrapped them carefully from the hoofs to the knees with bandages from the tack room. After that he just sat against the wall staring at Charcoal with unexpressed anguish. The black brushed the boy's cheek with his muzzle twice as if to thank him; then rested his nose wearily against the ledge, gulping in the fresh, cool air.

John Morgan had watched silently. Now he turned away. His voice was husky. "Peter, you're to tell me immediately if he gets worse, so I can call Doc Gray. I can't stay now, but I'll check with you every hour or so."

Peter nodded dumbly. He watched the gelding's every move, rubbing and rebandaging his legs at intervals. He filled the water bucket as fast as Charcoal emptied it. The black seemed to crave water and drank repeatedly.

Peter went to supper, but he didn't feel much like eating. He hurried back to the gelding's stall and took up his vigil. When Dr. Gray came about eight o'clock, he listened to Charcoal's breathing, sounded his chest, checked his throat and nasal passages, gave him more medicine, and took his temperature.

When he looked at the thermometer, the veterinary shook his head gravely. "Not so good. But then it's apt to be worse at night. There's nothing you can do for him now, son. Go get some sleep. It's possible Charcoal can get some sleep too. It would be good for him. Leave him a couple of buckets of water and check him once in the night."

Peter didn't want to leave. But by ten o'clock he was so tired he sat with nodding head; and several times dozed off, almost falling off the stool. His muscles were stiff and aching from being in the same position so long. Finally, with a goodbye pat for Charcoal, he went off to bed but set his alarm clock for three.

Three o'clock found slight change, although the horse had eaten a little. Peter went back to bed and slept through till seven. He hurried out before breakfast, realizing it was a weekday and he would be expected to go to school. Bob was just replenishing Charcoal's water bucket. The gelding nickered at sight of Peter, and the boy gulped. He went into the stall and noted the horse was breathing a little harder than the day before.

He sought out his father. "Let me stay with Charcoal. I think he's worse."

"No!" John Morgan's voice was firm. "The rest of us will check him every time we pass his stall. There's nothing you can do that we can't. Dr. Gray will be here after a bit; and if there *should* be a turn for the worse, we'll call you. Charcoal may be sick for days, and you can't stay out of school that long. Go along, son. We'll take good care of him."

Reluctantly Peter went off to school, but he couldn't concentrate on anything. He stared out of the study-hall window, worrying about Charcoal, wishing his father had never put the black out in the old shed, blaming himself for going to bed and giving up the search. The hours dragged endlessly, and at three-forty-five he was the first one out of the building and on the bus.

Peter ran all the way from the bus stop to the stable. Hastily dropping his jacket and books in the office as he went by, he headed for Charcoal's stall. Even before he reached it he could hear the black's labored breathing, and his heart sank. He threw open the door. Bob was kneeling in the straw rubbing Charcoal's legs. He looked up with a forced smile.

"Hi, Pete. Want to take over now? Better change your clothes first."

"He's worse, isn't he?"

Bob looked away. "I don't know. We'll find out when Doc comes again tonight."

Charcoal laid his hot muzzle against Peter's shoulder, and the boy hugged him gently. Turning quickly, he went out to the house and got into his jeans. Back in the stall he took over from Bob—wiping out Charcoal's inflamed nostrils, which were now draining a small quantity of mucus, mixed with blood and pus; replenishing the water pail; talking to the gelding in a quiet voice. Finally, when he had made him as comfortable as he could, Peter sat down on the camp stool, leaned back against the wall, and waited impatiently for the veterinary's evening visit. Charcoal seemed tired of standing—he was bracing himself against the side of the stall; yet he wouldn't lie down. Peter asked Dr. Gray about it when he finally came.

"A horse with catarrhal or bronchopneumonia like this . . . and, Peter, we have to face the facts; your horse *does* have it. No question about it now. As I started to say, a horse with this type of pneumonia persists in standing from the beginning unless he gets so weak he can't. Once down, he may not get up again. Try to keep Charcoal on his feet. I want you to give him hot applications; keep them up for three or four hours. Then rub the skin dry very gently, give him an alcohol rub, and fit a dry blanket over him

[157]

tightly. Try this once a day for three or four days if it seems to help. To keep him regulated, give him scalded oats, bran, or linseed mashes, and a warm-water enema several times a day if necessary. Will he stand for it?"

"I don't think he has the strength to resist anything now," Peter said ruefully. "I've been fixing him warm bran mashes, but he hasn't eaten much either yesterday or today."

"Give him anything he'll take willingly. Sometimes a sick horse will take a delicacy like corn on the cob when he'll refuse anything else."

The doctor administered two kinds of medicine. "I'll be back quite early in the morning," he promised. "I'll make this my very first stop."

"We've got a sling," Peter said suddenly. "None of us thought of it."

"Good! Use it."

As soon as Dr. Gray had gone, Peter sought out his father. "Dad, let's put the sling on Charcoal and fasten it to that overhead beam. It'll help hold him up and save his energy. He's getting weaker all the time."

John Morgan and Bob brought the big canvas sling and, with Peter caressing Charcoal and quieting his fears, they fastened it around his stomach and drew the overhead ropes, on pulleys, tight enough to support the gelding's body. Charcoal sighed wearily and sagged against the supporting canvas. He seemed to know they were trying to help him and made no fuss at all.

It was midnight before Peter would leave and go to bed. Comforted a little by the thought of the sling, he tried to sleep. At three o'clock he got up and replenished the water. Charcoal was no better.

For five days Peter kept an almost ceaseless watch over the gelding every moment he was not sleeping or in school. The hoarse respiratory murmur lessened. Peter thought it a good sign until the doctor told him it meant that the affected area of the lungs was becoming solid.

"When it begins to break up and absorb, you'll hear sound again—like bubbling or gurgling."

Peter stared at him with brooding eyes. "Tell me the truth, Doc. Will he get well?"

The doctor looked him straight in the eye. "He has a fifty-fifty chance. The next two days will give us the answer. There ought to be someone with him night and day now."

Peter stayed up all that night. His parents did not argue with him; but at six o'clock, when Bob relieved him, his mother made him go to bed, and she didn't waken him till nearly noon.

"Go on to school this afternoon," she said. "Tonight someone else will sit up with Charcoal."

That evening after supper Peter settled down on the camp stool. Charcoal stared at him with glazed eyes. His sides heaved as he gulped in deep breaths, and it was agonizing to hear him gasp. Peter worked on him almost ceaselessly—giving him inhalations of eucalyptus oil, as the doctor had directed; rubbing and bandaging, clearing out the reddened nostrils, and coaxing him to take a few carrots from his hand.

At eleven o'clock John Morgan appeared at the stall door. "Go and sleep," he urged. "I'll take over."

Peter stiffened. Even his father could not force him to leave Charcoal now. The doctor had said the crisis could come any time, that careful nursing was the all-important factor. He faced his father almost belligerently.

"No. Tomorrow's Saturday. I can't leave him."

John Morgan's hand fell on his shoulder with sudden respect and tenderness. "Peter, Charcoal's going to get well. He's got to. We're all with you . . . and him. From now on he gets the best stall in the barn, and this summer you're going to ride him in the big shows. I was wrong, Peter. I haven't been fair to you or Charcoal. I guess horses are in your blood the way they're in mine. I'll make it up to you. If you stay here tonight, I'm staying with you."

In spite of his anxiety a surge of happiness swept over Peter. His hand reached out to clasp his father's. All he said was "Thanks," but they both understood.

At three-thirty Charcoal seemed suddenly worse.

The mucous membrane of his eyes showed a distinct bluish color. The cough, which had been moist for several days, became more frequent and rasping. Father and son looked at each other silently, and John Morgan hurried to the office to call Dr. Gray up out of his bed. Peter felt himself grow cold all over. He rested a weary head against Charcoal's sweaty neck to hide the tears he could no longer hold back. By the time his father returned, he had gained a measure of self-control; but his throat burned and his hands on the gelding's legs were shaky. The one light left on in the aisle of the big barn cast ghostly shadows over the stall. The sound of the other horses moving restlessly about, champing their feed, or kicking fretfully at the walls, came dimly as from a great distance.

There was far more involved in this struggle for Charcoal's life than his love for the black gelding, great as it was. Peter had come to realize it in the long hours he sat alone in the stall. There was the long path of misunderstanding between him and his father that had preceded the storm; there was his own failure in giving up the search; there was his duty and obligation to Dodo, and his own future hopes for the gallant black.

The doctor came. Peter clenched his fists and waited as the veterinary worked silently and efficiently, doing half a dozen things he had reserved for just this moment of crisis if it ever came. At six o'clock, tired and disheveled, Dr. Gray took a temperature reading, laid his ear against the gelding's chest, listened carefully, and straightened up with a smile.

"The fever's broken. Absorption has begun. I'm sure he'll live. Peter, you've done a magnificent job of nursing. And so has everyone who helped you. It was double pneumonia—hard to lick. Go get some sleep now. Charcoal will be O.K."

Peter's knees felt suddenly weak with relief. He looked at Charcoal. The gelding gave a low nicker, the first in three or four days. Sobbing, Peter ran out of the stall to the house; and the two men looked at each other with a suspicious trace of moisture in their own eyes.

From then on, Charcoal gained slowly but surely. His appetite gradually came back. His legs gained strength and the sling was removed. Lungs, throat, and nostrils cleared up, but it was quite a while before his breathing came entirely back to normal. When the worst was over and Peter knew for a certainty that the gelding would live, he called Dodo on the phone. In those long hours in the stall fighting for Charcoal's life, he and the gelding had reached a perfect understanding. There was no longer any jealousy in his heart toward Dodo and her expert management of the gelding. Charcoal was destined to be a great horse. Who brought him ultimately to that greatness did not matter. He, Peter, had saved the black's life. Even his father admitted that.

Peter tried to tell Dodo something of what he had felt and experienced. He knew that she would understand, although she would be put out at him for not letting her know sooner.

"Doc Gray says we can ride him slowly a little each day, for exercise, in a couple of weeks, maybe sooner," he told her. "But it will be a couple of months before we can do anything strenuous, like training over the higher jumps. It will sure set him back for the summer shows. But he's alive and that's the important thing."

"I could shake you, Peter," Dodo said angrily. "You know that, if you had called me, I'd have come over and helped keep watch. It was exam week at our school, and I went back home this last week end again for Mom's birthday. Otherwise you know I'd have been calling you."

"I know," Peter insisted. "We *did* try to call you during the week end, but couldn't get you. It's just as well. We didn't want you staying up all night and all that sort of thing when you had to be in school all day. One was enough."

Eventually the jumping practice was resumed, and Dodo came over often to help. Pride rose in Peter every time he watched Charcoal sail over the barrier in perfect form. Dodo in the saddle was as much a part of the gelding as if she had grown there. Nevertheless, when Peter took over, it was always with excitement and anticipation. He worked Charcoal for an hour or two every day in order to give Dodo a rest and a chance to catch up with her school work. Then, a week before the show at the Academy, he phoned her.

"Will you ride Charcoal in the show? Everyone thinks he's strong enough to enter, if we don't put him over the highest jumps."

He could hear Dodo's gasp of delight and surprise. "Why, of course—if you really want me to. But I thought you were counting on riding him yourself. What's the matter?"

"Nothing," Peter retorted. "I have an idea about something; that's all. And, anyway, you do a better job with him over the jumps, and you know it!"

The night of the show Peter sat in the stands, pencil and paper in hand. His fingers fairly flew as Charcoal came proudly into the ring and flew over the jumps as if the devil himself were at his kneels. He was fast and in top form. He won easily over every jumper, stable-owned or privately owned. Peter studied the black intently, checking every detail of movement as he rose to each barrier; noting the clean lines, the sharply apparent joy he took in the jumping itself. He wanted desperately to get the spirit of it on paper and, oblivious of the crowd around him, he sketched rapidly.

He stopped momentarily to watch the judges hand Dodo the blue ribbon. He wanted to go down and congratulate her, but he had to finish while the image was bright in his mind. Satisfied at last, he thrust the paper into the back of the pad for protection and hurried down into the stable section.

Dodo was unsaddling, and she turned to him almost angrily. "Well! You sure took your time getting here!"

"You were swell!" Peter told her. "Look! Here's why I was so slow. Had to finish this." He thrust the rough drawing in front of her.

Dodo stared at it a moment, speechless. Then she turned to him, her eyes shining. "Peter, you've got it! This time you've really got it! No wonder you didn't want to ride!"

CHAPTER XVII

Peter Wins a Scholarship

After the show at the Riding Academy, there were few skeptics. Charcoal, in winning over even the veteran jumper White Eagle, had proved himself, and Peter found he was seldom without an audience when working the black over the jumps. One parent approached him with an offer to buy the gelding at a tempting figure for his teen-age son, and one of the Hunt Club members, an older man, put out tentative feelers on price. But Peter discouraged them at the outset.

He and Dodo worked together schooling the black on alternate days. Dodo had a long way to come on the bus after school. It was often six or six-thirty when she finished, so more often than not she had dinner with the Morgans.

"I hope you realize I wouldn't do this for anyone else but you and Charcoal," Dodo reminded Peter one evening as he walked her the two blocks to the bus stop. "Let's put him over the five-foot jump regularly now. I think he's about ready for it."

"O.K.," Peter agreed. "I'll bet he could do six feet if he tried."

"Whoa now," Dodo cautioned. "He's plenty good, but don't rush him."

The Civic Horse Show was to be held June the twenty-eighth. On the fifteenth Peter received a long, official-looking letter from the Northwest Art Institute, Seattle, Washington. When he pulled it from the rural mail box and saw the return address, his hand trembled so he could scarcely open it.

We are happy to inform you that you have won one of the scholarships given to Portland High School students this year. In the opinion of our judges, your companion drawings, 'Charcoal at Rest' and 'Charcoal in Action,' merited second-place award. The second drawing, particularly, showed remarkable life and realism. You are entitled to an eight-week summer course at our camp on Puget Sound completely free of charge. Board, room, and instruction from some of the West's finest art teachers will be furnished. You will be with nineteen other high-school students and our own adult students who attend the summer session. Recreation is provided, so that it is a combination vacation and

[167]

workshop. We feel this is an unusually fine opportunity and hope you will avail yourself of it. The session begins June 26th, and no late registrations can be accepted. Please wire your decision as soon as possible. We feel you have unusual talent and it should be encouraged.

> HENRY R. WORTHINGTON, *Director*
> Northwest Art Institute
> Seattle, Washington

Halfway to the house Peter stopped short. June the twenty-sixth! That meant he couldn't ride Charcoal in the Civic Show or the other three big shows he'd counted on in July and August. He couldn't expect to leave the camp each time, nor could he expect Dodo to do all the schooling and none of the riding.

For a moment Peter was tempted to keep the letter a secret, to answer that circumstances had changed and he was unable to accept. Yet deep down inside he knew that art was more important to him even than horses, and this same opportunity might never come again.

Yet . . . accepting meant he couldn't ride Charcoal all summer, and the black was just now coming into his prime. There could be many triumphs to be shared. Peter resolved to say nothing as yet and sleep on the problem. Night, however, brought little sleep, for he just kept mulling the matter over and over in his mind.

Then suddenly Dick's words came back to him: "Do you honestly like jumping? How can you expect Charcoal to put his heart into it if you don't?"

Peter faced facts. It had to be Charcoal and Dodo again for the whole season, with him rooting occasionally from the side lines. If he chose to go to the camp, could he be spared from the Academy for the summer? That was another problem. Although business was somewhat better, there had been a lot of expense with Charcoal's illness. His father had refused to disclose the total amount, had brushed it off with a statement that he would catch up with everything in time.

The next morning when he showed the folks the letter, they were delighted and insisted that he must go. Mrs. Morgan hugged and kissed him happily, to his considerable embarrassment. His father looked proud and only asked if he had enough money put away for his bus fare. Dodo, when he called her up, went into ecstasies. Peter wondered if part of her joy was due to the fact that she would get to show Charcoal.

"Maybe your Dad won't let you come and ride that often," he said.

"Peter, would you consider letting me take Charcoal back to the farm again after the Civic Show? You know Dad trucks his horses around to all the major shows in the Northwest. I'd be able to be with the folks, yet Charcoal would get around to lots more shows than if you were showing him yourself. We'll keep enough of his winnings to cover expenses. Dad wouldn't care because he's as crazy about Charcoal as I am. Please say yes. We could even take him to the biggest event in the Northwest, the Championship Show in Seattle, August nineteenth and twentieth and you'd get to see him there. Please!"

Her voice was cajoling. Peter gave in. "O.K. But you and your Dad sure do a lot for me."

When Peter left for camp, he made Dodo promise to send an air-mail letter with the results of the Civic Show. The bus trip to Seattle was uneventful. There Peter met the other nineteen scholarship winners, and they were taken on to the camp in a chartered bus. It was a beautiful spot—a colony of well-built tent houses in the pines, with a central lodge hall and dining room.

By the time Dodo's letter came saying that Charcoal had done himself proud, taking a first in one class and a second in the other, Peter was well adjusted to the new routine. He liked his instructors and his three roommates. He and the instructor-adviser had had a friendly conference in which he was advised to broaden his interests and draw a wide variety of subjects if he expected to succeed in commercial art. Although he enjoyed drawing horses twice as much as anything else, Peter knew the instructor was right and resolved to try.

The next six weeks literally flew by. They were punctuated with letters from his family, all of them cheerful and with no hint of the anxiety about money Peter knew they must be feeling. Dodo's letters came every ten days or so, long and chatty, filled with detailed accounts of Charcoal's latest exploits. He was winning consistently, practically never out of the ribbons, and had garnered an impressive total of points awarded by the Northwest Horse Shows Association. He seldom failed to take the blue, and Peter read avidly the flattering newspaper accounts that Dodo clipped and sent. He could not help showing them and bragging just a little about Charcoal to his tentmates and other friends. Soon Charcoal was almost as well known around the camp as Peter was.

Then came the big news he had been waiting for. Dodo wrote that the Hayneses were all coming to Seattle for the Northwest Championship Show in August. The Haynes stable would have five horses in the show, and Peter was to look for their stable quarters just as soon as he arrived. The camp director consented to his being gone for the last day of the show. The important jumping classes would be held them.

Summing it all up, Peter found that Charcoal had been shown in twenty-four classes at sixteen shows during the current season and had garnered seventeen firsts, including three silver trophies; four seconds, three thirds, and almost a thousand dollars in cash— several hundred of which had gone for entry fees, feed, stall rent, and a share of the transportation. This, together with his ribbons and cash winnings of the preceding season, made the black gelding one of the top six-year-olds in the West. Thrilled as he was over Charcoal's success, Peter realized that most of it was due to the Hayneses.

He salved his sense of obligation with the knowledge that Dodo was enjoying it thoroughly.

CHAPTER XVIII

Top Show

It would be grand seeing the Hayneses again, Peter thought as he rode along on the bus. This summer was the longest he had ever been away from home and, although he hadn't been actually homesick, he was mighty happy now at the thought of seeing friends. He arrived at the show grounds about an hour before the afternoon performance, and as he rounded the corner of the long row of stalls he ran straight into his father.

John Morgan grabbed him by both shoulders. "Hi, son! It's mighty good to see you."

Peter could hardly believe his eyes. "Dad! I didn't expect to see *you* here. Nobody told me. Is Mom with you?"

"Didn't expect to be here myself. But Mr. Haynes' trainer blew up and went off yesterday, leaving him high and dry. Dodo and her Dad couldn't take over *all* the work. Bill Haynes wired me and I drove up to pinch-hit. Brought your mother along, and Dick Stearns too. Dick said he had to see Charcoal or bust.

[173]

You'll find them when you go up to the stands. Here's your reserved-seat ticket."

"I haven't seen Charcoal yet," Peter reminded him, "or Dodo."

"O.K. They're on down the line five or six stalls. Right now I've got to meet Mr. Haynes in the show office for a conference. See you later."

Peter hurried on and found Dodo grooming Charcoal in Stall No. 6.

"Hi!" Her face lighted up. "How does it feel to be the owner of a near-champion?"

"Swell." Peter just stood and looked at the black for a few minutes, too moved to speak. Charcoal nudged him gently. He rubbed the gelding's forehead and studied him from head to tail. Charcoal looked wonderful. His eyes were bright, his mane soft and silky; his black coat glowed with a mirrorlike sheen.

"Here!" Tactfully Dodo thrust a brush and currycomb into his hand. "You give him the finishing touches while I go over to the van and change into my riding clothes."

It felt good to be grooming a horse again . . . especially Charcoal. The black turned his head and butted at Peter, as if to say hello again. When Dodo came back half an hour later, resplendent in her hunt costume, Peter helped her saddle up, gave Charcoal a last encouraging pat, and reluctantly sought out his seat in the grandstand.

As he threaded his way through the narrow aisles to the section pointed out by the usher, he caught sight of Dick Stearns and Mrs. Haynes . . . and next to her, dressed in her Sunday best, his mother. Peter slipped into his seat beside her—to be met with a smile and greeting from Dick and Mrs. Haynes and a hearty kiss from Mrs. Morgan.

"Peter," she said. "It's good to see you! Are you going to surprise us with Charcoal today?"

"I don't know," Peter said cautiously. "I sure hope he's as good as usual. I've been looking forward to this for weeks."

"Well, how do you like the camp?" Dick asked.

"It's swell. Wish I could go every summer." Peter pointed suddenly to the ring. "Look! Here come the horses."

The first two classes were soon over. Mr. Haynes, who had been riding in one event, joined the others in the stand. Charcoal was not entered till the third class —the open jumpers. When he won first place and the blue ribbon, Peter was in seventh heaven. The gelding had jumped consistently and in perfect form. Dodo had ridden him superbly. Watching them, Peter knew once and for all that they belonged together.

The last class of the day was marked on the program "Special event—to be announced." Peter wondered several times what it could be, but he halfway forgot it as each class performed brilliantly and gave way to the rest.

"They're all so good," he remarked wonderingly. "I'd sure hate to be one of the judges."

"It's a championship show," Mrs. Morgan reminded him. "These are the winners from all over the Northwest. You can be mighty proud Charcoal's in such good company."

Dodo and Mr. Haynes rode in some of the classes, returning to the stands in between. Peter's father rode in the others. The stable was doing very well indeed—in spite of the fact that two new horses were strange to John Morgan, and he to them. Charcoal showed in one more class—an obstacle course, winning second.

"Well, that makes your horse eligible for the Open Championship," Mr. Haynes told Peter.

There was a peculiar note in his voice. He opened his mouth as if to continue, then closed it and watched Peter with a half-smile on his lips. Peter didn't notice. Charcoal had already won championship at smaller shows, but this was different. As the Open Championship came closer, his excitement mounted higher and higher. After what seemed an interminable period the gong sounded, warning the riders to get ready for it.

Mr. Haynes rose. "I'm riding Gray Girl," he said quietly, "since our trainer left us in the lurch. Dodo will be on your horse, Peter. May the best horse win."

Peter gasped. It had never occurred to him that Dodo might be riding against her own father or that

Charcoal and a Haynes entry might be pitted against each other for the championship. Gray Girl would be no mean foe. Peter sat forward tense and embarrassed. He hated to look at his mother or Mrs. Haynes. Suddenly his mother leaned over and touched him gently on the arm. Peter felt better.

"First entry in the Open Championship," the announcer called out over the loud-speaker system, "Gray Girl, owned by the Haynes Farms; ridden by the owner, William Haynes."

Gray Girl was off to a splendid start. She topped the first jump easily, landing with a catlike grace that did not even jar her rider. Then she was up and over the four-foot bars so quickly that Peter could hardly follow with his eyes. The five-foot barrier, a brush jump, was next. Perhaps the gray would find it just a bit more difficult. Wanting her to make it, yet afraid she would, Peter saw her rise flawlessly and clear it with a good six inches to spare.

"Well!" Mrs. Haynes leaned over and spoke to Peter. "Charcoal will have to go some to beat Gray Girl. She's in perfect form today. But, Peter, we all want the best horse to win. Dodo's only fault is that she sometimes lets a horse rush his jumps too much. Let's hope she doesn't do it this time with Charcoal."

There was a sudden shout from the crowd. Gray Girl had topped her last jump, the five-and-a-half-foot bars, with only a light tick to mar an otherwise clean record.

Peter settled back in his seat with a sigh of disappointment. With competition like this, how had he dared to hope that Charcoal could win? He began to worry about whether Dodo would keep calm and hold the gelding down. At best, he might have a chance at second place. Number Two, a small brown mare veteran of many years of competition, did beautifully on the first three jumps but tired on the fourth and knocked down the top bar. Peter knew she had seen competition in three earlier classes and was not surprised. She was a game little jumper, ably ridden by a boy about his own age; so he joined in the applause when she left the ring.

Number Three, a tall, lanky chestnut, refused twice on the third jump and was ruled out. Yet earlier he had scarcely been faulted in three different events. Peter shook his head, answering his mother's query with a puzzled frown.

"I don't know why that was. Maybe just tired, maybe temperament. I sure hope Charcoal's in the right mood."

"He's been pretty consistent lately," Mrs. Morgan reminded him. "Have faith in your horse, son. He needs it."

Peter was silent, a trifle ashamed. He *did* have faith in Charcoal; but Mr. Haynes, with all his years of experience, was a better rider than Dodo, and Gray Girl was a wonderful horse. It had been nip and tuck for two seasons between her and Charcoal when it came to piling up the wins. If only Dodo remembered to hold Charcoal back, give him a chance to collect himself easily and thoroughly for each jump! He could see his father back in the line-up, talking earnestly to her.

Number Four, a Thoroughbred stallion, did almost as well as Gray Girl, except that he had two ticks, one each on the last two jumps.

"Unless one of the last three entries turns in a clean score, Gray Girl's the one for you to beat," Dick remarked, trying to relieve the tension. "Here comes Charcoal."

The black's satiny hide shone in the August sun. He arched his neck and moved onto the track with a pride of bearing that was a far cry from the rangy, awkward three-year-old of the Horse Heaven country. Dodo was a picture in her formal black hunt costume with its jaunty velvet cap. She sat her mount very straight and slender, in perfect balance. Peter felt a lump come into his throat.

"Looks mighty pretty, doesn't she?" Mrs. Morgan said softly. It was uncanny how she seemed to guess his thoughts.

"Yep, and it's swell of her to ride for me against her own Dad. But I sure hope she holds Charcoal down."

The first jump was child's play for the black. He

cleared it almost contemptuously. Dodo was holding him to an easy gallop. Peter drew a sigh of relief. The second and third jumps Charcoal also took in his stride. Then he seemed to falter momentarily. Peter drew in his breath with a gasp. Had he imagined it, or for just a moment or two had the injured tendon played Charcoal false? He seemed to detect a momentary break in the smooth motion. But no one else had noticed it; and the gelding was fast approaching the final jump, again in perfect rhythm.

Peter found himself shouting suddenly, although he knew Dodo would never hear him. "Take it easy! Take it easy!"

For Charcoal's speed had increased a little too much. His timing was off; and this time when he took off for the jump, there was an almost imperceptible catch of that hind foot. Peter went up and over the jump every inch of the way with Charcoal. He didn't hear the click of a hind shoe against the bar. He was too intent on getting the black down and onto the course without injury. When Charcoal made a smooth recovery and eased off into a collected canter with no trace of a limp, Peter sat back and felt weak all over. In spite of the tick, he was sure Charcoal had at least tied with Gray Girl. So nervous he could hardly sit still, he watched the other three horses take the course with varying degrees of success. Not one turned in a perfect score; only one even approached

Gray Girl and Charcoal. Peter was not surprised when the judges called the gray and the black back into the ring.

"There will have to be a jump-off between Numbers One and Five," the speaker boomed out. "Raise the final jump to six feet, please."

Peter gasped. Two or three times on the practice course Charcoal had cleared six feet, but never in competition. There had been that tiny suggestion of a catch on the injured tendon. Peter rose suddenly and pushed his way frantically to the aisle. There was no time for an explanation to the others.

He heard the announcer saying, "Number One will jump first. Number Five please wait outside the gate."

Thank heaven for that! Peter ran down the steps, almost falling in his haste. He dodged around corners and through openings in the crowd. Ducking under the rail, he crossed the track above the course and doubled back at top speed, his heart pounding in his chest. He practically flung himself on his father, who stood near the rails.

"Stop Charcoal! Withdraw him. I think he's strained the bad tendon. We can't take a chance!"

John Morgan stared at Peter. A sudden look of pride came into his eyes.

"I thought I saw him falter too," he said. "You're right, son. No championship is more important than your horse."

Quickly John Morgan stepped up to the judges' stand and spoke hurriedly to the senior judge. All three of the judges turned incredulously. They seemed to argue for a moment; then the announcer was called over.

Tensely Peter waited. He scarcely saw Gray Girl clear the six-foot jump and come down to earth without a fault. Then the loud-speaker demanded attention.

"Ladies and gentlemen—a sudden change. The owner of Charcoal, Number Five, has withdrawn him from this class due to an old injury and the fear of endangering the horse's future. The championship therefore goes to the great mare, Gray Girl, owned by William Haynes. She has just turned in a faultless performance. Our congratulations to the Hayneses . . . and to the Morgans as well."

Dodo reined Charcoal back from the gate unbelievingly. For a moment she just looked at Peter and his father, her face stricken with sudden and bitter disappointment. Then her eyes brimmed over, and she slipped from Charcoal's back. Peter took the reins and she brushed by silently, not speaking to him.

"I'm sorry," Peter muttered awkwardly. He felt relieved when her father rode through the gate with the blue ribbon and Dodo went over to him.

Mr. Haynes jumped off and took her in his arms. "It was the only thing to do," he said. "And it was mighty brave of Peter. You wouldn't want to take a chance with Charcoal either, would you? I saw him break his stride, and I was afraid for him too. I know you love him as much as Peter does."

"More!" Dodo choked out. "It's all right. Only I know he could have cleared that jump too, just as good as Gray Girl."

"Maybe. But then there would have had to be another jump-off, and neither you nor Charcoal would have been up to it. Gray Girl had been ridden in only one other class. Get back on. They're calling you into the ring for your ribbon."

Dodo wiped her eyes with her father's big handkerchief and let him boost her into the saddle. She tried her best to smile as the judges handed her the red second-place ribbon. The crowd gave her and Charcoal a tremendous ovation as she rode the gelding twice around the ring.

"Just a moment!" One of the judges called as she reined him toward the gate. "Remain in the ring, please."

Puzzled, Dodo drew rein. The judges gathered in the stand, busily conferring. Silence settled over the crowd as everyone waited to see what was the matter. Dodo was embarrassed. She rode the black gelding slowly about the ring while Peter and the two older men leaned against the railing, wondering.

Then suddenly all three judges came out to the center of the ring. One of them carried a magnificent silver cup. The announcer leaned over the microphone.

"Ladies and gentlemen, you know that this is a championship show—a show for the outstanding horses in the Northwest; horses that have won at least three blue ribbons and one championship in recognized shows throughout the area. This year we have set up a new award. As you know, under our Northwest Horse Shows Association, points are awarded for each ribbon won in member shows, with extra points for championships. This year we are awarding, through the kindness of Bailey's Department Stores, this beautiful trophy to the northwest jumper with the largest number of points won in a single season.

"With the winning of the red ribbon just awarded, Charcoal, owned by Peter Morgan of Portland, tops his nearest competitor by four points. We therefore take great pleasure in awarding the trophy to him, and the title of 'Champion Jumper of the Northwest.' If the owner is present, will he come forward, please."

Through a mist of happiness Peter felt himself literally pushed through the gate by his father and Mr. Haynes. He and Charcoal met halfway across the ring. The judges handed Peter the giant cup amidst thunderous applause. Peter took the cup and handed it up to Dodo. Smiling happily, she circled the track while Peter stood and watched. Then he grasped the bridle reins and walked at Charcoal's head off the track and through the gate. Passing the row of owners leaning across the rail, Peter suddenly glimpsed a familiar face. It was Wilson Parks, the owner of Black Beau. The rancher raised his riding crop in a hearty salute.

"He's Beau's son," he said. "No doubt about it now. The old boy will be mighty set up when I go home and tell him."

Peter smiled proudly.

CHAPTER XIX

Peter Sells a Horse

John Morgan took the reins. "I'll go load," he said. "You'll want to see the folks."

Peter was glad he was going. "Dodo," he said suddenly. "Go on up to the stands, please, and tell the others we'll meet at the stable where Dad's packing up. I want to talk to your father."

Dodo looked at him curiously, but she did as he asked. Before Peter could approach Mr. Haynes, two men accosted him. "Come here a minute," one of them said, drawing Peter aside. The second one went right along, much to the other's disgust.

"Look," the first man said confidentially. "I'm Henry Williams. Operate a big show stable out of Van Nuys, California—jumpers especially. I'll give you three thousand for that horse of yours, spot cash."

Peter gulped. Three thousand for a horse that had cost him thirty dollars! "He isn't registered," he said. "We don't know for certain that he's a Thoroughbred."

"I don't care if he's part Pekingese," the man insisted. "That horse can jump. That's all I care about. As for that injury you spoke of, I've made my inquiries. Find he's been jumping steady now for two years with no sign of it. I'm willing to take my chances."

"I'm sorry," Peter told him. "I can't let you have him."

At that the other man stepped forward. "I couldn't help hearing. I'm Joe Graves, trainer for the Millrun Stables, Boise, Idaho. My boss is after just such a horse, and I'm authorized to pay up to thirty-five hundred dollars. What do you say to that?"

Peter stared at him. It was somehow very confusing that everyone wanted Charcoal so much. "No," he said, "I can't sell him to either of you. He's already promised."

Suddenly Mr. Haynes stepped forward. He had been watching and had heard enough to guess the trend of events. He caught Peter's eye with a question. Peter nodded slowly.

"Yes," Mr. Haynes told the other two firmly. "I have first option on the horse—at four thousand dollars."

"O.K., he's yours," the first man muttered. He turned away.

The second stood irresolutely. "If I were to raise the ante? Say forty-one hundred?"

"No," Peter repeated. "I tell you, he's sold."

The trainer walked away disgustedly.

Dodo's father laid a hand on Peter's shoulder. "Did

you mean it, Peter? Or were you just wanting me to help you out of a tight spot? I've wanted to buy Charcoal for Dodo for a long time; but I didn't say anything because I know how much you think of him, and I didn't want to high-pressure you. If it hadn't been for your careful early training, he wouldn't be where he is today."

Peter swallowed. "I want you to have him, Mr. Haynes. I was going to offer him to you after this show, no matter what happened. I wouldn't sell him to anyone else, but to you it's different. I've known for a long time that Dodo should have him. With her and him it's just like with me and Star. I guess I just hated to admit it. He couldn't be where he is today without you and Dodo either, and I know it!"

"I'll make out a check right now." Mr. Haynes pulled out his pen and walked over to the railing. "Is four thousand dollars O.K. with you?"

"It's too much," Peter protested. "You know he isn't worth that. I've never paid you enough for all the care and training you've given him. You practically own an interest in him now."

"No, look, Peter. You're all wrong. Charcoal has already won close to fourteen hundred dollars in prize money in two seasons. With proper care and good judgment such as you showed today in withdrawing him when the going got rough, he'll easily have ten more years of jumping competition. Figure that out for yourself. Anyway you heard what those fellows offered. They both drive a hard bargain and one was prepared to go much higher. I think I'm getting him cheap at four thousand dollars. As for his care and training . . . you paid for it, and you know Dodo's had twice the money's worth in enjoyment and thrill of winning with him. You've been very generous with her, Peter. But let's get this deal concluded." He smiled. "I want to be sure you don't change your mind."

Peter stood silently while he made out the check.

"I'll fix up a proper bill of sale when we get home and mail it to you to sign," Mr. Haynes said, handing him the check. "Your father should sign it too since you're a minor." He flung an arm around Peter's shoulder. "Well, let's go and tell Dodo the big news."

As they approached the Haynes stable quarters, they saw considerable activity. Dodo was packing up the tack while the stableman rubbed down the horses and John Morgan blanketed them and loaded them into the big van, one by one. They would make Portland that night; stable the horses at the Academy overnight, after turning some of the rent horses into the ring to make places for them; and go on home the next day, ending one of the most successful show seasons in their existence as a stable.

Mr. Haynes hurried forward to where John Morgan was loading the horses. Charcoal still stood in his stall, peering out at them. Peter wondered whether he should tell Dodo the big news, but he decided not to spoil it for her father. He didn't look at Charcoal. After all, he was sixteen now and to cry would be sissy. His father and Mr. Haynes were talking fast and earnestly. Peter waited impatiently. So much important news to be told . . . and no chance to tell it! At last Mr. Haynes came back to Dodo. Peter lingered in order to see her face when her father told her. But without a word Bill Haynes went to Charcoal's stall. He snapped a lead rein into the black's halter and led him out, straight to his daughter. As he passed, Peter let his hand trail along the glossy hide—feeling the warmth of the gelding's body. He turned away for a moment.

"How would you like to put your own horse in the van?" Mr. Haynes inquired.

A look of incredulous joy swept over Dodo's face. "Mine! Dad! You're not fooling? You don't mean . . ."

"Yes, I *do* mean it." Mr. Haynes handed her the lead. "I've just bought him from Peter. We'll call him a birthday present, even though your birthday *is* a month off, and we'll board him at the Morgan's Riding Academy for the next four years until after you finish senior high school, so you'll be able to keep yourself and Charcoal in jumping trim. Summers you can show him."

Dodo threw herself into her father's arms.

Peter hurried over to *his* father. He pulled the check from his pocket. "Dad, I just sold Charcoal to the Hayneses. I'd like to keep about a thousand of this to get me started in commercial art school after I finish senior high. I want to pay back the cost of Charcoal's bout with pneumonia; and the rest I want you to take for the Academy, to catch up with the payments. If you won't take it as a gift, call me a partner in the business—Morgan and Son."

He hurried on before his father could protest.

"I know what you're going to say—that the money's mine. But it's practically all profit, and I couldn't have had Charcoal all this time if you hadn't let me have my way. I was pretty much of a heel about it sometimes too. And I'm just not cut out to do justice to a jumper, although I hated to admit it. He's been Dodo's horse from the first time she set foot in the stirrup. You know that I've got more than a thousand dollars clear from Charcoal's winnings and, with that and this thousand, I can easily earn the rest of my way through art school."

John Morgan smiled. There was a new light in his eyes when he looked at Peter. "I've made a lot of mistakes in handling the Academy these past two years—thinking I could do it all myself without sufficient variety of experience. And I've been so worried at times I haven't been fair to either you or Charcoal. One of my biggest mistakes was letting Dick

Stearns go. This has always been mainly a hunting and jumping stable, and business has fallen off sharply without Dick's help. Now that you have offered this money, the firm of Morgan and Son is rehiring Dick. I feel that things are going to go better for us from now on."

Dick, who had stood smilingly in the background, suddenly stepped forward. "You know I've saved quite a bit this past year on the job. I'd like to put some capital into the business too, if it's O.K. An addition on the stable quarters can mean more steady boarders; more advertising will bring more business; there would naturally be more profit." He turned to John Morgan. "As good as you are with horses, I'd hate to see you give up the stable now. Together the three of us can make a go of it, I know. How about it?"

The weariness and discouragement that had etched itself deep on John Morgan's face eased as if by magic. "I'm sure we can work something out," he told Dick. "Why, just the prestige of having the North-west's champion jumper stabled at our place will draw a lot of customers." He put a hand on Peter's shoulder. "After all, it's your horse that turned our luck."

Peter grinned happily at Dodo. "You know, Carrot Top, I'm not exactly sorry you and Charcoal will be around for the next four years. And no one can ever call him a 'broomtail' again."